My Ex-Boyfriend is My Next Boyfriend

By: Allie Marie

Chapter 1

Tracey

Five Years Ago...

"*Tracey, you looking at ten years. Help me, help you. You can walk away from this with a clean slate and continue your life. All you have to do is tell us who the drugs truly belong to," said the prosecutor, Jones.*

"*You're trying to help me, huh?" I said, looking at this lady like she was crazy. Not even a half hour ago she had gotten my bail denied, now she talking about she's trying to help me. Please.*

"*I see this happen all the time. It's one of the reasons why I hate my jobs. I see innocent women all the time trying to prove their loyalty to their boyfriends or husbands, and as soon as they start their sentence; they leave them high and dry. Look at you. They will eat you up in jail. You trying to be this ride or die chick and it is not a good look for you. You come from a privileged background. You never struggled a day in your life. Now you're telling me that you're ready to throw all of that away for some low life thug?"*

"*Ms. Jones, it's not your job to help me. It's your job to put people away. If you truly wanted to help me, you wouldn't have gotten my bail denied."*

"*May I speak to my client alone for a minute?" My lawyer asked, who was also my uncle Brandon, my mother's brother. Uncle Brandon was one of the best criminal defense lawyers in the state of Pennsylvania.*

"*Sure, I just want to say one thing before I allow you your time with* the counsel. We know the drugs belong to Mason."

"Privacy, prosecutor," Uncle Brandon said with some base in his voice to let Ms. Jones know he wasn't playing. As soon as Ms. Jones walked out, he started talking.

"Tracey, what are you trying to do? Do you want to win this case or take the bid? Let me know because we are wasting time going back and forth with this lady. We know who the drugs truly belong to. Now, I'm going to be honest with you, that whole thing was a setup. They have you on camera since the time you pulled up into the parking lot. Mason has been doing business with an undercover cop. The only thing is, he would always send females to the meetings. He never went to any of the drops himself. They only have him on the phone calls, but all of the numbers can never be traced back to him. So, they truly don't have any real evidence on him, and the night that they were supposed to meet up with him, you were the one that showed up. They need you to testify against Mason to have any type of charges brought against him. But, right now, they don't have a case on him, and they can't even build one with the evidence that they do have."

"Uncle Brandon, what do you want me to do?" I asked. Confusion was an understatement.

"I'll tell you to testify against him. Mason is a punk, and no real man will send women to do a man's job. On top of that, you have so much to lose. Think about your future. You have a full ride to Temple University. Your parents are very important people in the city of Philadelphia. Are you willing to continue to embarrass the people who gave you everything you need? The ones that worked hard to make sure you would never want for anything and make sure your life was nothing like theirs growing up? Now the question is, are you willing to break their hearts and say fuck you to your future for some nigga who didn't even bother to show up to your bail hearing?" Uncle Brandon hissed, shaking his head.

Everything he was saying was true, but Mason was the love of my life.

"Yeah, Uncle Brandon. I understand everything that you are saying, but Mason will never snitch on me if the shoe was on the other foot. I can't do this to him. I wouldn't be able to live with myself. I choose to make this drop for him. He didn't force me to do anything. You know he's already a two-time felon, and what they're trying to make me do, it will probably put him in jail for the rest of his life." My voice cracked as tears came to my eyes.

"Time's up. I am a very busy woman. Now, what is it going to be Ms. Harris? If I were in your position, a seventeen-year-old young lady being charged as an adult with a bright future ahead of me, I would put my freedom first. We know the drugs belong to Mason, and Mr. Mason didn't even hesitate to tell us that the drugs belong to you," Prosecutor Jones stated with a smirk that I wanted so badly to smack off.

"Mason said he never talked to yall. I don't know who you trying to trick with your little mind games, but I know as much as you do that you spitting a whole bunch of bullshit."

"Well, since you think you have everything all figured out, why don't you sign this plea deal. You will have a mandatory five and will be eligible for parole with good behavior. Either way, I think your lawyer will agree there's no reason to stretch this out. I'm pretty sure Mr. Brandon Harris, your lawyer, informed you that there's no way to get out of this without giving us what we want. However, I rather give you the plea deal because you have already embarrassed your parents enough. I wouldn't be surprised if the careers they worked so hard for don't start to crumble because their daughter is going to be a convicted drug dealer and trafficker."

Looking over to my uncle for reassurance, he leaned in and whispered in my ear, "I can't help you if you don't want to help yourself. If we take this to trial, we will lose. There is way too much evidence against you without giving them what they want. Plus, you put your parents through enough."

Trapped wasn't even the word that could've explained the way I was feeling at the moment. I felt like the world was on my shoulders. No matter the decision I made I would be hurting someone that I loved.

I knew I was breaking my parent's hearts by putting Mason's life and freedom before my very own. I was their baby girl, born with a silver spoon in my mouth. Both my parents had very successful jobs, causing me to never want for anything. I never saw myself going to jail, shit, I'd never even been to prison to visit anyone, but love would make you do some crazy things.

Here I was, about to lose my full scholarship to Temple University and my future. But I loved Mason too much to rat on him. We figured since I was only seventeen years old and still considered a minor in the state of Pennsylvania that I would be charged as a juvenile. Clearly, I was wrong. I guess they felt coming after me as an adult; it would make me break and tell on Mason. My parents and uncle wanted me to make a deal with the prosecutor. However, I couldn't seem to do that to Mason.

"I'll sign the plea deal."

Present Day

"Yo, I can't believe I'm finally out," I muttered as I waited for the huge steel gates to open. The warm summer breeze hit me in the face, and all I could do was smile. I could've been over exaggerating, but the air felt different being on the outside of jail.

Standing by the car was my two best friends, Brooklyn and Riley. They held me down throughout my five years in the pen. They were all the family I had besides my cousin, Reign, and my ex, Angelo. Without them, I wouldn't have known how I would have made it through.

"Hey boo!" Riley yelled, running to me, hugging me.

"Wassup y'all? You don't even know how much I missed y'all."

one today.

"Well, enough about them. Let's talk about Angelo. You know he told me to call him when we picked you up," Riley said, changing the subject

"Yassss! Let's talk about Angelo's fine ass. That's the nigga you need to be worrying about. The real nigga that held you down," Brooklyn said.

"I know. That's bae, for real." I smiled, thinking about Angelo. Even with our crazy break up, he was still my everything.

"That's good to know. Now call him before he snap out on us. He was already feeling some type of way because we wouldn't let him pick you up from prison," Riley said, handing me over a brand-new iPhone X Plus

"This mine?" I asked, taking the phone from her.

"Yes, Angelo bought it. He said don't worry about the bill; he got it." Brooklyn made sure to add that little information.

Ring. Ring. Ring.

"They finally let a real one out. How you feeling, ma, being free and shit?" Angelo's deep voice came through the phone. I swear, just hearing his voice had me leaking like a faucet. Five years and no dick would drive any girl crazy.

"Yes, and I'm loving every minute of it. Thank you for my phone."

"No problem. You already know I got you," Angelo stated. His voice was calm and soothing. There was no doubt in my mind that whatever I needed Angelo would help.

"What you about to get into?"

"The girls about to take me to Reign's, to get pampered. You know I need it."

"You deserve it and much more. Don't worry about anything. I got you for whatever you need."

"Is that right?" I asked.

"You should already know but let me get off the phone and handle some business. Enjoy yourself, ma. Call me when you finish. I'm trying to see you."

"Umm, not tonight, playboy. We're going out!" Brooklyn yelled into the background, causing Angelo to chuckle.

"Tell Brooklyn she drawling, trying to keep you, hostage," he fussed.

"Oh, I see you trying to get some fresh out jail pussy. Okay, Lo, I see you."

"Yo, I'm out. Ya girl crazy. Riley is the only one with some sense," Angelo said through coughing. I could tell he was smoking and Brooklyn no filter ass caught him off guard with that statement.

"I know. I been saying that all of the time," Riley co-signed.

"Call me later, shorty," Angelo told me.

"Okay, I will," I said, not really ready to get off the phone, but I had no choice because he hung up after he heard my response.

"Girl, you need to let Angelo dig in those guts tonight after we go out. I know ya ass need some dick. It's been five years."

"Brooklyn, stop," Riley said, busting out laughing

"Bitch, whatever. It was nothing wrong with my fingers while I was locked up," I admitted with no shame.

"You got it. Knowing my bi ass, I would have become a full-blown lesbian." Brooklyn said.

"Man, some bitches were always trying to get at me. I was always fighting in the first couple of months. Shit, I wasn't having that. I can't get down with the bumping of coochies."

"Right. It's nothing that would make me go that way, but no judgment, though," Riley agreed, shrugging her shoulders

"Look, bitch, don't knock it until you try it," Brooklyn said, sticking her tongue out.

An hour later, we pulled up to my cousin Reign's Day Spa. I was very impressed. My cousin was doing the damn thing. Reign and I weren't blood cousins. She was my mother's best friend daughter, and after her mother's death, my mom had no problem being a mother figure in her life.

I was proud of her. And if you knew her life story, you would've thought she would've turned out to be some government statistic. However, she beat the odds that were stacked against her. Reign was the type of person that motivated people like me. No, she had never been to jail, but she witnessed her father murder her mother at the age of fifteen. She sold drugs to survive, but that only lasted for about a year before Sean, Angelo's brother, claimed her as his. Sean was the person she was selling the drugs for.

When she fell in love with Sean, he made sure she never had to stand on the corner to sell drugs again or needed anything from anybody. Now that was a couple to admire and idolize. Everybody wanted relationship goals like Beyoncé and Jay-Z, but Sean and Reign was the couple you needed to be like. It was sad to see their love come to an end when Sean was murdered on her twenty-first birthday. Till this day, I was surprised she had found love again.

Reign was so loyal to Sean that it took her forever to move on, but now she's engaged to the one and only, Pharaoh Black, and they shared a set of beautiful twins.

"Hey boo," Reign said as soon as I opened the car door. She was beautiful standing there glowing. She looked so happy standing next to a man who I assumed it to be Pharaoh with the way he was just tonguing her down in front of her Spa.

"Hey!" I said, getting out of the car. Reign smiled as she rushed over to me, embracing me with a hug.

"I'm so happy that you're home. It's been a long five years."

It seemed like it had been forever. I swear I didn't want to let her go. It was crazy when time got real; I saw the people who was really going to be in my corner. My time in jail told me who was real and who was fake.

"I know, right," I said happy that it was finally over.

"Babe, this is my cousin the one and only, Tracey Harris. Tracey, this is the man who stole my heart, Pharaoh."

"Wassup, ma? Welcome home. Ya cousin told me so much about you," Pharaoh greeted, giving me a hug. I couldn't even deny; Pharaoh was fine as fuck. I saw why he had my cousin so smitten.

"Reign, you don't see us over here?" Brooklyn said, smiling, making their presence known.

"Hey B," Reign said, mushing Brooklyn playfully before speaking to Riley.

"Hey, Riley, baby."

"Hey, Reign," Riley said, giving her a hug.

"Wassup y'all? Babe, I'm out. Make sure you close early like I told you. I have plans for us." Pharaoh grabbed Reign and pulled her in for another kiss.

"I wish you would tell me," Reign whined. She hated surprises, and always wanted to know.

"Just finish up here. I'm not telling you. Come home so we can finish what we started in your office before we leave." Pharaoh tried to whisper the last part, but we heard him.

"Okay."

"Bye Pharaoh." Me, Brooklyn and Riley all sang and waved, bye. He smirked and said, bye, back to us.

"Alright, bitches, don't be drooling over my man. I'll cut a bitch over that one," Reign threatened, jokingly.

"I'm just saying. It should be a sin to be that fine," Brooklyn stated, causing Reign to laugh. I was pretty sure this wasn't the first time women had gawked over Reign's man.

"Come here, Tracey. Let me talk to you. B and Riley, you can go get ready for y'all session," Reign ordered.

"Wassup, cuz?" I asked as soon as I walked into her office.

"Look at you all in shape." She admired my body.

"All I did was work out. Did yoga and meditate to get my mind straight."

"Well, you look good. Where are you staying?"

"On the real, I didn't even think about it honestly. I guess I can stay with Brooklyn until I get on my feet. You know Riley live with her fiancée, and I don't want to impose," I answered. I honestly didn't think about my living arrangements. I was just so happy to be out.

"Yeah, I feel you. But you know I have a few rental properties around West Philly. You know I can rent one out to you." The smile that she was wearing on her face when she offered me a place to stay had me looking at her sideways. It was almost like she knew something that I didn't.

"Rent? Reign, I don't have a job," I stated the obvious, looking at her like she had lost her mind.

"Angelo already paid the rent up for a whole year. And, the job part, you can become the new receptionist, if you want. No pressure but I know the job would be a good look for your parole officer."

16

"Wait, What?" I was totally confused, not thinking I had heard her correctly.

"You heard me. Lo setting you up lovely. He rented you one of my properties, a three-bedroom house with two bathrooms, and a garage. And, you should have already known I was setting you up with a job period. Now you just need to try to get back into school. Tracey, you have a fresh new start."

"I know, and yes I want the job. Thank you so much. It seems like you and Angelo making my adjustment back to society an easy one. You know I will not let you down." I couldn't help but smile, truly blessed to have them in my life.

"I know you won't. Tracey, have you talked to your parents yet?" Reign asked the million-dollar question. My parents were a sore subject for me.

"No," I let her know, feeling sad that I hadn't talked to them in five years. I truly wished I could turn back the hands of time, but that was not the way life worked.

"Well, believe it or not, but your mother has been checking on you through me. Also, she has been putting money on your books while you were in prison."

"I tried calling her and my father while I was locked up and my calls went unanswered."

"They were in their feelings about you choosing Mason's bum ass over your future, and eventually them. Your father is one of the best brain surgeons at the Children's Hospital of Philadelphia, and your mother is the best real estate agent in the Tristate. They worked hard to give you the life you had, and you fucked it up over some nigga that didn't give a fuck about you." Reign said, speaking nothing but the truth.

It hurt me that my decision had disgraced my parents. They didn't even care about what their peers thought of our situation or me, but I hurt them when I didn't choose the right way.

"I'm not a snitch." was the only thing I could say that could justify my actions.

"I feel you. I live by the same code, too, but no real nigga is going to let you take a bid for him. A real man wants to make sure his lady succeeds in everything in life. Mason got crab syndrome. He will pull others down so that he could come up on top. He knew what he was risking when he got into the game. So, don't try to hold a grudge against your parents who held you down without recognition, but you want to reach out to Mason for some bullshit closure." She snapped, shaking her head.

"I already told you why I needed closure from him in my letter." I shot back. I hated the way Reign, Brooklyn, and Riley was making me feel like I was crazy for wanting to close that chapter in my life. Sure, maybe I should've just left well enough alone, but there was so many questions running through my head that only he could answer.

"Yeah, I know, but I don't agree with you though. I say fuck that nigga. What you need to be doing is checking for Angelo."

"I know." That made me smile.

"I can't believe he did all of this for me," I then said, still in shock. That man made sure I came home not wanting for anything.

"Yeah, and he did this for you with no strings attached. Lo is the real MVP," she said, causing me to laugh

"That's my baby for real. I'm just scared," I admitted. Even though Angelo was always honest with me, he did cause me my first heartbreak, which led me to dating Mason.

"Scared? If you don't take your scary ass on somewhere." Reign laughed.

"All I'm saying is, Lo is the man. Bitches doing anything to get his attention, and the nigga only have eyes for you. Don't fuck around and miss out on a real one because of some insecurities brought on by a weak ass nigga."

Did I have insecurities? The answer to that would be a yes. I was the picture perfect girlfriend. I was loyal, and yet niggas seemed to mess with other bitches. Just hearing how the women were falling all over Angelo made me want to fall back. I didn't have time to be risking getting locked up again for beating some bitch's ass.

"Listen, you don't understand..."

"You're right, but it's your life, Tee. All I want you to do is to be happy and not have any setbacks. This is your fresh start. Make the best of it. Now let's get you pampered." Reign said her peace and her changing the subject let me know; she would never bring it back up. I could take her advice or leave it, but I knew she would support me every step of the way.

closest people next to him were suffering. Shit, Mike was already locked up before they started touching real money."

"Long story short Mike asks for Sean and Blue to look out for Mason. They did, but Mason was a natural born fuck up. When my brother and Blue put us on, they tried to put Mason on too. This nigga got caught with a pound of weed and some pills. Mason ended up only doing six months' in prison when he was eighteen. The second stent was because he violated his parole, he had to finish out his sentence. He barely survived that little bid in prison without the protection of GMM on the inside. So, when he came out, my brother tried to keep his word and look out for Mason. So he gave him easy jobs that he couldn't fuck up. But he started doing some shit on the side and ended up getting his girl at the time locked up. So, we jumped his ass out… the only reason why he still alive is because of Sean and Blues' loyalty to Mike." I finished, and Majesty nodded his head.

"I just wanted to bring this to y'all attention. Handle it in due time but not tonight. It's Ira's birthday. Plus, ain't nobody trying to hear Pharaoh's mouth about y'all fucking up his establishment." Majesty said, and I nodded. Mason may have gotten a pass tonight, but best believe he will be receiving a visit from me soon.

Chapter 3

Mason

"How you get a meeting with Pharaoh?" Austin asked looking around the club, watching everybody enjoying the music and liquor.

We were currently in Pharaoh Black's club 'Royal.' Tonight was going to be a good night. Me and my team had an important meeting with one of the Black brothers. Doing business with them is an honor and privilege. If you're trying to make a name for yourself in this street game, it's no better way than to do it with the best.

I had a good feeling tonight. I had the bottles popping and the bitches trying to get into our V.I.P section. Me and my team were looking like money, and that's the perception I wanted the Black Brothers to see.

"Yeah what time is we supposed to meet up? We been here for two hours and nobody hit you up yet." Peanut asked looking at me sideways like he didn't believe I set up this meeting.

"Yo, what the fuck is your problem?" I barked over the loud music, getting in his face.

"Chill ya hostile ass out. I just want to know how you pulled this so-called meeting off with Pharaoh. When it's a well-known fact that the Black Brothers only fuck with G.M.M in Philly." Peanut said in a matter fact tone, pissing me the fuck off. Lately, he has been questioning my every move and authority.

"Our meeting is with Majesty, and I told him we're apart of G.M.M. and we're looking to branch off and do our own thing," I explained.

"Why the hell you say we're G.M.M?" Austin asked, shaking his head. In my eyes my plan was solid. So, what I embellished the truth a little. At least I'm making moves to get me and my team feet wet in the game making some money.

"Because, I am apart of G.M.M! My brother started G.M.M along with Sean and Blue. I dare somebody to come at me sideways for using that name to get connections. Shit, I should be the one running GMM. Not Cream and Angelo and whoever that other nigga Ira is. He's only running shit because he related to The Black Brothers. Angelo just has a personal vendetta against me because I took his bitch."

"So with all that to say, you mean to tell us you have set up a business meeting with the legit brother? That nigga not into the street life," Peanut muttered in total annoyance.

"So the fuck what! That nigga is my way in period. Who the fuck do you got trying to put us on." I snapped. Peanut always had some slick shit coming out his mouth but didn't have any connections to put us on.

"Nobody," Austin answered.

"Exactly!"

"Man, you got us looking like some muthafucking snakes. You don't think Majesty going to tell Angelo and them about this secret meeting?" Peanut hissed.

"Instead of coming to him like a real businessman you came to him ready to do some shady shit behind one of his business partners back." Honestly, I didn't look at my actions like that but looking at it from Peanuts' perspective it did come off as grimy and disloyal.

"Well, what's done is done. At least we got Majesty's attention." I said trying to justify my actions. Shit, I'm an optimistic person. The Black Brothers can see this as an opportunity to expand and bring in more money.

"Hey, babe" Desi walked into our section cutting our conversation short. Which I was happy for the disruption I was tired of explaining myself.

"Wassup?" I responded pulling her down on my lap and kissing her neck.

Desi is my wife and the mother of my son who neither of us take care of. We weren't meant to be parents we all about the come up. Making money moves was all we had on our minds. She was actually the one who was able to get me in contact with Majesty. She works as a stripper at KING's, so she was able to get his number from one of the security guards that work there.

"Damn, GMM is in here deep, looking like a bag of money." One of Desi friends, Lisa, said. This bitch was staring across the club with money signs in her eyes.

"I know right." Desi smiled giving Lisa a high five causing me to push her off me and onto the floor, with her sack-chasing ass.

"Bitch take y'all hoe asses over there than." I snapped. Not only did she say what she said, she said that shit in front of my niggas. How can I be a leader and my girl out here acting like a straight hoe and disrespecting me in front of my face?

"Shit, you don't have to tell me twice. Desi and Gianna are yall coming? They have enough females up here to make them look good and keep them company," Lisa said with no shame in her game. Looking into Desi eyes as Lisa helped her up off the floor, I could see she truly wanted to go across the club and party with GMM. Gianna had already stood up ready to leave our VIP section.

"Mason, calm down. The way GMM partying and drinking. A couple of them would be an easy lick." Desi explained.

"You're always scheming." Austin chuckled shaking his head.

"Those niggas *are* in here deep. You pick a perfect time and lyn her number on a napkin.

"Do y'all want to join them," I asked my girls. I knew tonight was supposed to be girl's night out and I didn't want them to think I wanted to ditch them to be with Angelo.

"Hell yeah," Riley said, throwing her shot back then took mine and Brooklyn's.

"Damn," Brooklyn said looking in shock. Riley is the most responsible and designated driver, but it looks like she needed to unwind.

"Listen, I just want to have fun because I know as soon as I go home it's going to be World War III in my house," Riley admitted.

"Welp, let's turn up baby," Brooklyn said. We learn a long time ago when it came to Riley and her relationships to just be a listening ear. As long as Sebastian's not physically hurting her, then we keep our comments to ourselves. Riley was the type of person who had to find out for herself when it was time to let go.

Angelo met me as soon as we reached the VIP section. All eyes were on us as we made our way to his section. It was no word said between me and Angelo as he pulled me into him and kissed me passionately. It was like he was staking his claim and I didn't mind.

"They let a real one out." Cream said walking up to us and gave me a hug as soon as Angelo let me go.

"Wassup, Cream?" I smiled.

"Damn, who is this fine ass nigga," Riley muttered staring down this handsome dark skin man walking their way with a bottle of Dusse in his hand.

"Tracey, this is the homie, Ira. Me and him did time together." Angelo said, introducing us.

"Welcome home, ma," Ira said hugging me.

"Thank you. I heard so much about you." I said as he nodded, but his eyes were no long on me, they were on Riley and Creams on Brooklyn.

"Who are ya friends?" Ira asked, walking up to Riley.

"Well, that's Riley and Brooklyn. Riley and Brooklyn, this is Cream and Ira." I said.

After the introductions we all started to have a good time. Riley was so wrapped up in Ira you wouldn't think she was actually planning a wedding with Sebastian Taylor Jr. and Brooklyn was just being her living carefree self flirting with Cream. I did notice the dirty stares from some of the other females. I guess Reign was right. Angelo was a hot commodity.

"Brooklyn!" Someone called B's name.

"Lisa! Gianna!" Brooklyn called back to them. "Can my girls come up here?"

"Yeah," Angelo answered.

"Come on y'all…. Oh, wait a muthafucking minute!" Brooklyn said, stopping her friends from entering the section.

"I know y'all heffas didn't think she was coming in with y'all."

"B, what's the problem," I said standing up and walking over to where Brooklyn was with Riley right on my heels.

"There's no problem. Lisa, I'm cool with y'all, but I don't fuck with that bitch and y'all know that. Tonight is about my girl and we needs no drama."

"Damn, five years flew by quick. Look who they let out of the state penitentiary." A voice that I would never forget said.

"Bitch, I know you lost ya damn mind," Brooklyn yelled, reaching for Desi.

"Chill, Brooklyn. This bitch still in her feelings but she trying

At this point, I just wanted peace and positivity coming my way. Karma is a bitch, and I believe Mason will get what's coming to him. My closure was seeing Mason and Desi together. That only proves I was never anything to Mason. I came to the realization after losing five years of my life, but now I think I just made peace with my reality and past choices. This was a lesson that I will have to chalk up to game. The rest of the right was a blur as we got fucked up, and party hard. I just silently prayed that I made it to my parole meeting on time.

Chapter 5

Brooklyn

"Up next is the one and only, *Honey*. It's Friday night, and I know some of y'all done cashed your check and is ready to pay all her bills. I heard she taste as sweet as her name, too." The DJ Rock announced, as I made my way to the stage. Dressed in a gold glitter G-string and matching pasties stripper heels. Looking out into the audience, a smile crept up on my face as I saw men and women surrounding the stage, pulling money ready to make it rain.

She working Onyx, but she say it's only temporary

It's been 3 years, and she's still here, and I was gettin' scary

Say she don't wanna dance forever, I look at her with my face like,

Why? Why?

She super sexy everybody wanna know about her

The one that everybody want but no one clever got her

Because the way she get it in, all of the men, even the women,

all try, all trying

Neyo's voice blasted through the speakers. Neyo's song *Love the Way You Move* was speaking volumes to me right now. Instead of working at Onyx, I was going on my fourth year at KING's. At KING's I'm known as Honey and the number one money maker. When I'm on stage, I get into my own little world as I allow the music to take over my body. My hips always put my audience in the trance, and I wind my hips slowly to the beat. Climbing up the pole I showcased my new routine as I did multiple flips and swing around the pole seductively.

Girl if this club was the sky,

You're the brightest star

You ain't playing fair sliding down that pole like

What? Drop a couple stacks on you that's nothing

Hundred after hundred girl a nigga ain't fronting

You ain't in the club then I ain't coming

Say she's tired of all that bullshit

Gonna quit the game, change your life and ease your pain

Hold up, work so hard it's time to play

Baby girl take it off for Trey

Swinging on the pole, I could barely see the stage as it was filled with so much money. Looking at all of the money on the floor let me know I was doing my damn thing. My set was coming to an end as I slid down the pole landing in a split and started to make my ass clap.

"Damn Honey!" DJ Rock said shaking his head as he watched my ass bounce up and down. It had him hypnotize.

"GMM in the house tonight. Welcome home, lil Corey!"

Hearing GMM being shouted out made me look around the club, and I came face to face with Cream as he walked up to the stage. It was like time stood still as I watch him throw two stacks of neatly hundred dollar bills, still bonded together in rubber bands, onto the stage. I don't know why at the moment I felt embarrassed by my career, but the way his eyes was looking through me made me feel ashamed.

Maybe it was because me and him have been talking for the past two weeks since we met at club Royal. I quickly tried to

42

gather my money into my money bag, only for all of it not to fit. One of the bottle girl's came with a trash bag so I could put the rest in there. Once I collected all of my paper, I quickly made my exit to stage left.

"Damn, Honey, did everybody give you all of their money," Lisa asked with a hint of attitude.

"Naw I'm pretty sure I ain't empty out everybody's pockets." I laughed. I know they was salty but no need to be. I already told King I was only staying for a couple hours before I headed home. I had school in the morning. Spring semester was finally coming to an end and finals were only next week.

Yeah, you heard me right a bitch was in school. I was currently attending Temple University getting my bachelors in Nursing. Shorty has goals. I wasn't the typical stripper. As a matter of fact, I was only doing this because it paid the bills and my tuition. I'm currently debt free and that's because of KING's. I didn't come from a family like Tracey and Riley. Their parents were married and actually loved one another. My father was a pimp, and my mother was his bottom hoe.

I grew up having a father's love and a mother's hate.

My father Harlem was born and raised in New York, and my mother Rochelle was a Philly native. The story that was told to me by one of his many hoes is that I was the only person my father loved. That was the reason why my mother hated me. I received the love that she long for from my father. When I was young, my father took very good care of me. I know he would be turning over in his grave if he knew I was out here being a stripper. He never wanted this life for his one and only child. How hypocritical of him.

He didn't want me out here doing anything degrading like stripping, but he didn't have a problem putting someone else's child on the stroll.

I barely seen my mother, either. She was working the streets, or she avoided me like the plague. My father was murder when I was seventeen. His funeral was the first time I seen my mother in years. And it wasn't a pleasant sight. Instead of being loving and caring she basically told me I was on my own. Rochelle didn't have a motherly bone in her body. She was a foster child and ran away from home at the age of thirteen and been selling her body ever since.

At fifteen she got pregnant with me. She was my father's favorite girl, but it was only because she made him the most money. With my father's untimely death Rochelle uses that as her way to get out of the life she was living. All I was to her was a constant memory of what her life use to be. From what I hear now she's married to a preacher down in Augusta Georgia, and she's playing step mommy to his children.

Harlem's mother, Diamond, told me my father's house was paid for and all I had to do was pay for the utilities and taxes. She didn't care that I was seventeen, either. In her eyes I was an adult. Diamond already raised her kids, and she wasn't going to start over raising me. Diamond kept it one hundred and told me I should never be broke if I have a pussy. So, I finished high school while working at Macy's in King of Prussia Mall. I wasn't going to be selling pussy so when I decided to get my life together and settle down my pussy hole was as large as Lincoln Financial Field. The field where my beloved Philadelphia Eagles play, but as soon as the opportunity presented itself I definitely signup to do the next best thing.

As soon as I turn eighteen, I met Strawberry, and she told me to come to her job KING's. They was hiring bottle girls and strippers. I first went for the bottle girl position and was making some nice money. It was enough to pay my bills and keep me dress in labels. But after one month of working as a bottle girl and comparing what I was making in tips to what Strawberry was bringing in, I did what I had to do and started to strip. After my first year, I stacked about sixty thousand dollars from KING's and traveling doing private parties. I knew I didn't want this to be my life forever. I see how this industry destroys lives and breaks women. I knew I had to do something, so I enrolled in school with much encouragement from Riley, and Tracey in the many letters she wrote. I enrolled to get my degree in nursing.

I want the real thing one day. Real love the love I see when I look at my homegirl Reign. She was lucky to find that unbreakable love with Sean and Pharaoh. Shit, I want that Will and Jada love and that Obama and Michelle type of love. I honestly crave it. Every time some man or woman sees me, they see Honey. Maybe that's why I tried to hide what I do from Cream. He was cool, and it seemed like we just clicked. But I know I can kiss any chance we ever had goodbye. His whole team just saw me strip. Shit, I got most of their money in my moneybag.

"You're leaving?" Sunshine asked walking into the dressing room.

"Yeah girl finals coming up and I have to study. I made my bread I'm going to be on my way." I said as I changed into my Victoria Secret sweat suit and slid on my Ugg slides.

"It's more money to be made GMM making it rain on all of the bitches," Sunshine said laughing, as she started twerking.

"Y'all got it.!" I slapped her ass and before grabbing my duffle bag that contained my money, clothes, heels and, make up.

"Alright, Honey, I'll catch up with you later. I'm trying to be like you and only have to work a couple hours not all night." Sunshine said before she made her way out the door. I chuckled, and followed her lead, walking out the front door to wait for my Uber. I never drove to work I heard too many stories about some of the customer following the girl's home. Still, I have my license to carry and I will never be too afraid to pop somebody in the ass for trying me.

"What he say?" I heard a familiar voice. Looking over to the side, it was Mason and Desi that bumped me, storming out the front door behind me.

"I'm fired because of ya old hoe. Who the fuck knew Reign was fucking Pharaoh!" She said damn near in tears. "Plus, he said he not letting me work because you on some snake shit. And because my teeth fucked up."

"Watch where you walking, bitch." I snapped just to get under her skin. She whipped her head around so fast I thought she was going to get whiplash.

"Don't start ya shit." Desi snapped. All I could do was stare, and my mouth hit the floor. Angelo crazy ass really knocked out her front two teeth.

"Fuck it! KING's not the only strip club in Philly." Mason muttered as Desi continued her way to the car. All I could do was shake my head.

"Those clubs not bringing in money like KING's," Desi hissed at Mason before they both got in the car and pulled off. As I watch them speed out of the parking lot almost hitting the car that was coming in, I realize it was my Uber.

"Brooklyn?" The Uber driver said after he rolled down the window.

"I know ya ass not about to jet without speaking to me." Cream's voice boom out of nowhere, causing me to stop dead in my tracks.

Chapter 6

Cream

"**B**ruh, she's good," I said to her Uber driver and handed him a one-hundred-dollar bill for the inconvenience.

"I'm okay," Brooklyn assured him as he gave her a look as to silently ask her was she okay after taking my money.

"Nigga, I said she was good! I should take my fucking money back!" I barked, causing him to quickly put his car in drive and pull out the parking lot.

"Stop being mean," Brooklyn said before she burst out laughing.

"Take a ride with me," I demand more so than asked.

"I guess I have no choice since you sent my Uber on its merry little way." She rolled her eyes but followed me to the car. Opening the door for her, I saw her face twist in surprise.

"What, a goon can't have manners?" I asked looking her dead in the eyes.

"No... Thank you." She muttered before I shut the door and walk to the other side to get in and start the car.

"No problem."

Tonight, I was showing love to one of my soldier's lil Corey. He just came home from doing a little stent upstate. Of course, GMM was bringing in his homecoming like no other than with music, liquor, and bad bitches. There's no other place to do that better then KING's. So imagine my surprise when I saw Brooklyn damn near ass naked swinging on the pole. I can't even lie shorty had every man and female's attention in the building.

Brooklyn, or should I say, Honey, had me captivated. I dropped five thousand dollars on her alone. The thing that threw me for a loop is that I've been talking to shorty ever since the night we met at Club Royal. She never let me know that she was out here shaking her ass for some cash. What she told me was that she was in school to be a nurse.

"So, do you want to address the big purple elephant in the room or continue silently to my unknown destination?" Brooklyn said with a hint of attitude.

"You're the one who has some explaining to do," I responded coolly. I wasn't going to pressure her into telling me wassup. If she didn't want me to know that part of her life, then I will respect her wishes.

"Where are you taking me?" she inquired, quickly changing the subject.

"I'm taking you to one of my little spots."

"So, I guess that's another way of saying you taking me to a spot where you entertain ya hoes?" She asked I could feel her eyes burning a hole through the side of my face.

All I could do was laugh because I was definitely taking her to a spot where I entertain my female guest. Nobody knows where I lay my head at if you ain't my mama, Angelo or Ira. You don't know where I really live. A nigga have trust issues. I've seen the closest people to a person be their downfall. So, I'm good on letting people in on a personal, trusting level. But I did use this place or when I didn't want to drive to my house out in Radnor, Pa. If I wanted to stay in the city, I use this condo.

"Naw, this is my little spot I stay at when I'm in the city," I answered, telling her the half-truth.

"Ummm hmmm," Brooklyn muttered and sat quietly in the passenger seat until we reached our destination. Once inside Brooklyn had a look of approval plastered all over her face, as her wandering eyes looked around the condo.

"This place is really nice." She complimented

"Thanks. You might as well get comfortable because we chilling tonight."

"Sawyer, are you telling me or asking me to stay with you tonight?" Brooklyn asked, calling me by my government. I don't even know why I told her that shit.

"Don't call me that." I hissed. I don't know what possessed my mother to name me that shit. But here I am Sawyer Lewis Jr. named after a muthafucka who won't look in my mother direction because she had me, instead of getting an abortion. "And I'm telling you because I'm not driving ya double life having ass back across town."

"I see you have jokes." She placed her duffle bag next to the sofa.

"Sike naw... I've wanted to chill with you for the longest. Are you hungry?"

"Yeah, I can eat. What you ordering?" She asked.

"Ordering? Girl you done took all of my money. I'm about to heat up this spaghetti I made yesterday and pop some garlic bread into the oven."

"Cool. Can I use your shower," Brooklyn asked.

"Yeah down the hall to the right."

While she was in the shower, I heated up the spaghetti and put some garlic bread in the oven. Twenty minutes later Brooklyn decided to waltz her ass back into the dining area in nothing but one of my white tank on, stretching it all out to cover all of her curves.

I could tell she was as naked as the day she was born underneath the shirt. Her nipples were poking out, and the shirt stopped just under her ass.

"Damn you couldn't wait for me?" Brooklyn asked with her hands on her hips. I would have shown a little more hospitality if she didn't have my shit brick up the way she did. I'm tempted to fuck around, get up and bend her little ass across my table.

"Ya plate in the microwave." I watched her hips sway side to side as she struggled to pull the shirt down a little before retrieving her food.

"This looks good. I'm mad you started eating without me."

"You were taking forever in the shower. You probably done used up all my hot water." I joked, and she laughed.

"That was a quick shower for me, and it was only twenty minutes. I don't know what type of bird bathing bitches you use to dealing with, but I ain't one. I take hygiene very seriously."

"Man eat your food," I said shaking my head. Her mouth was reckless. I already knew by the end of the night I was going to get her in check.

"But I want to explain to you what you saw tonight at the club." She started.

"I think it was evident what I saw tonight at the club. My thing is why lie and jet the fuck off the stage like I was about to beat ya ass or something."

"I don't know... I guess for the first time ever I felt ashamed." She admitted, putting her head down.

"I'm not one to judge anybody. I see you doing what you need to do."

"I mean I never been embarrassed or ashamed before. Stripping provides a comfortable life for me while I go to school. I'm debt free. I don't have any student loans and my bills are paid. It's just, I

50

didn't want for you to know that side of me. I wanted to be more than Honey the stripper. I wanted to just be Brooklyn."

"But Honey is a part of Brooklyn and if no nigga can see you doing what you need to get ya paper than fuck em," I said honestly. At least she wasn't out here tricking or setting niggas up. My motto is fuck everybody's opinion when it comes to a person's personal life. "Shit, ain't nobody else taking any student loans out for your ass. Or pay ya way through school.so don't you ever allow somebody to make you feel ashamed."

"So, you'll be okay if your girl was stripping? What if I was ya girl could you look pass my occupation? Like ya whole team just saw me shaking my ass damn near naked." She asked.

"If I had a girl, which is a strong, if, because I'm not the relationship type, my girl wouldn't be stripping because I got her. But if you were my girl what happens before we were together is just that. Everybody has a past," I said with a definite tone. Brooklyn was cool as shit, but I wasn't the settling down type and I didn't want her getting any type of mix signals thinking we can become more than fuck buddies.

"Thanks, it's good that I know you're not judging me." Brooklyn said as she finished eating her food. We had general conversation about life and everything you would do when you try to get to know somebody. When we finished eating she collected the dishes and started to wash them by hand.

"You know I have a perfectly working dish washer." I asked.

"Yeah, but it's like five dishes. It won't kill me to wash them by hand." She chuckled.

I knew I probably shouldn't have crossed this line with her. *Yeah let me take my ass in the other room. I'll fuck shorty whole world up with this dick.*

"I'm all done," Brooklyn said standing in front of me while I was sitting on my couch.

"Good," I muttered grabbing the back of her legs and gently pulling her on top of me in a straddling position. I was losing the internal battle I was having. Brooklyn was cool, and I didn't want to mess up our friendship because I couldn't keep my dick in my pants. And, if shit turns left I damn sure don't want to hear Tracey mouth about me playing her girl. Then again who walks around in a man house with nothing but one of his white beater on and not expect to get dick down.

"You seem tense. We're both grown, and I want some dick. No strings attach. Just two sexual people consenting to give each other multiple orgasms."

With that being said, Brooklyn slid off my lap to where she was standing in front of me again. Taking off the white beater, my mans instantly sprung to life. My eyes were fixated on her perfectly size melon breasts as they travel down to her flat stomach and ass, which was more than a handful to grab. She slowly lowered herself onto her knees and pulled my grey Nike sweats and boxers down.

"Damn," I heard slip from her lips as she looked in amazement at my length and width.

"You sure you can handle him?" I asked and silently prayed she knew what she was doing. There was nothing more than a turn off when a bitch can't suck dick. Granted I'm a big muthafucka so deep throating is something she may not physically be able to perform, but don't be sucking my dick like you scared of it.

"Trust me, I got this."

Within seconds she was placing me in her mouth. And she took as much as me as she could. I was surprised when I hit the back of her throat and she hadn't gagged yet.

Brooklyn was turning out to be a freak as she was sloppily sucking the soul out of me alternating between my dick and balls. Shorty had my head spent as I tried to think about everything under the sun to keep from cumming early. The game changer was when she grabbed her breast and placed my dick in between them. The sensation I was getting as I titty fucked her and she was still sucking my dick at the same time had me ready to throw all caution to wind.

"Fuck," I groan through gritted teeth to keep from screaming out like a bitch. I ain't never cum this hard. You could hear my toes cracking as I released my seeds into her mouth only for her to swallow them.

"It seems as though I took care of little daddy just fine." She boasted as she held my limp dick with two fingers. I couldn't even say shit back because shorty definitely handled her business.

Picking her up, I laid her on the couch. I usually don't give head, but I couldn't allow her to show me out like that. Pushing her legs all the way back to her head only for her to lock them behind her head, by her ankles, giving me the perfect view of her pussy, who juices was already leaking. Diving face first I was sucking, licking and French kissing her clit. Grabbing her waist, I lifted her up only a little to gain access to start eating the booty like groceries.

"Oh... my... God! Cream," Brooklyn screamed as she started squirting all over the place. But I wasn't done. It was like her nectar was addictive. I continued until she let out another piercing scream of pleasure as her juices erupted like a volcano.

Thank God for leather couches, I silently thought as I unhooked her legs from the back of her head.

"Come on let's go to the bedroom."

"I can't move." she whined. "My legs feel like noodles." Picking her up, I threw her over my shoulder and made my way to my bedroom and laid her down on my king size bed. There was no tapping out tonight. She was about to get this long dick.

Bang! Bang! Bang!

"Who the fuck banging on my door?" I muttered, forcing myself to get up only to find myself in the bed alone.

Where the fuck is this girl? I silently thought looking around the room. Before grabbing my grey sweatpants and putting them on. I noticed my condo was silent with no sign of Brooklyn. Her damn duffel bag wasn't even next to the couch.

This bitch done dipped out on me.

Grabbing my gun under the coffee table I walked to my door, swinging it open I aim the gun at my unwanted guest.

"Cream! It's me," Jodi screamed with her hands up in front of her face. Seeing her in front of my door made me want to snap. Jodi was some shorty I been fucking with on and off.

"What the hell you doing here and why ya crazy ass banging on my door like you lost ya fucking mind?"

"I'm not crazy.... You the one answering the door with grey sweats. Dick swinging like you just hopped out some pussy, waving a gun. Now get that shit out my face."

I put my gun by my side. Jodi was looking like she was damn near in tears as she looked at me. I already knew she was about to say some crazy shit.

"Jodi, why are you here?"

"No, the question is who the hell was that bitch sneaking up out of here doing the fucking walk of shame at six in the morning?" I was so thrown off by her question. Like, how did she know when Brooklyn snuck up out of here?

"I know you weren't camped outside of my house." I asked. This is the main reason why nobody knows where I truly live.

"What.... Wait, I was her Uber driver." Jodi quickly said, but I knew she was lying due to the fact that she was looking everywhere but at me.

"Bitch, stop lying you wasn't her fucking Uber driver." I was calling her bluff.

"So the fuck what Cream! Who is that bitch?"

Shaking my head, I couldn't even deal with Jodi crazy ass at this moment. I just slammed the door in her face, only for her to continue to bang on my door like a mad woman.

"Stop banging on my door before I shoot ya dumb ass," I yelled, and she knocked two more times before everything went completely silent. All I could do was chuckle as I thought about Brooklyn and how she definitely dipped out on a nigga. At least I didn't have to come up with an excuse to get her the fuck out of my spot.

Chapter 7

Desi

"What the hell, Peanut!" I hissed as I felt his sperm cover my face.

"What?" He asked as he continues to jack himself off until he jerked himself dry, while holding the back of my head so I couldn't move. All I could do was allow him to disrespect me.

"You said you wasn't swallowing."

"Nigga, that don't mean give me a facial like I'm some hoe!" I was pissed. Did he really think what he did was acceptable?

"Shut your crybaby ass up," he spat, throwing me a wash towel to wipe my face.

"Are you going to give me some money, or what?" I asked, getting dressed.

"I shouldn't give you shit. You still fuck with that nigga Mason. Not only did he allow some muthafucka to knock ya teeth out, he can't even afford for you to get ya grill fixed," Peanut said, throwing me a couple of stacks. My eyes lit up like a Christmas tree.

"I see you got money to blow. You can't say the same for ya team," I said. I wanted to know how he was getting money.

"That's not my team. I'm not fucking with Mason. That nigga going to get us killed the way he moving. If Austin was smart he'll get out too. Austin has a whole degree. He better put that shit to use. As for me, I'm working for my cousins Law and Aquil. They are selling guns that are more of my speed anyway."

"It's messed up that you can't even put ya boys on. Mason always looked out for you. We supposed to be family." I was trying to get Peanut to see how it's fucked up for him to be eating and everybody else struggling.

"Naw, what's messed up is you bandwagon for a nigga who played ya dumb ass to left when he met Tracey and then only started fucking with you because ya cousin put him on."

As much as I hated to admit it, what Peanut said was true, and still to this day that truth hurt. Mason was my man and he dropped me like a bad habit when Tracey came around. At first, he tried to play it like he was just getting under Angelo's skin. That didn't make any sense to me because Angelo and Tracey were never a couple to begin with.

What hurt the most was that I could tell he was really falling in love with Tracey. That's why I started sleeping with Peanut. The only problem with Peanut was that he didn't have the connections I thought Mason had. His brother was one of the founding members of GMM. When my cousin Pookie told me about his connect, I got back in Mason's good gracious by putting him on.

Money was flowing, and his little Tracey didn't have nothing on me. I was once again the number one lady in his life in my opinion.

"Well, I took care of Tracey dumb ass for about five years." The words slipped out of my mouth so fast that I couldn't even stop myself.

Fuck!

"What you mean you took care of Tracey?" Peanut asked, giving me that look that told me I better not lie.

"Well, lets just say I knew what was going down that night she decided to make the drop. Two days before the dro,p I went to visit my cousin Pookie upstate. He told me how he got caught up and that his connect was actually the DEA. He was only letting me know because I was the one making the drops. He told me to tell Mason, but instead I convinced him to allow Tracey to make the drop. Long story short, the bitch took the bid for him and I ended up with my husband."

There, I said it! I been holding that truth in and honestly, it felt good to let it out. Call me what you want, but I did what I had to do to protect me and my nigga. There was no way I was going to hand deliver Mason to the DEA. The way I look at it, I handled two problems at once. If I need to do it again, I will.

I could feel Peanut eyes burning a hole through me. Looking in his face, I couldn't even imagine what was going through his mind, as his face appeared emotionless.

"Say something."

"You're a fucked-up individual; knowing you did some snake shit like that, I can't even fuck with you," Peanut said, snatching the money he just gave me out of my hands.

"Why you so mad? She wasn't ya bitch!"

"Desi, you set that girl up on some get back shit. The fucked up part about it, she didn't even know you and Mason was ever together. All she knew, your ass was one of Mason's business partners. Shorty didn't deserve that, and she lost five years of her life over some jealousy. On top of that, do you know the niggas she connected to is crazy? If the truth ever gets out, you can consider ya self dead." He said, and I knew it was true.

Angelo already knock my front two teeth out. That was because I said I was pressing charges. I know if they ever found out I set Tracey up, my family would never find my body.

"How she going to find out when you're the only person I told? The only other person who knew what I did is my cousin Pookie, and he's not snitching."

"You don't have to worry about me saying shit. Just keep ya

distance from me. You're not going to be able to escape your fate much longer. Karma is a bitch," Peanut said before walking to his front door and opened it. I couldn't believe the way he was acting.

"So you really just not going to help me fix my teeth?" I asked, hoping that my little confession didn't make me lose my chance of him paying my dentist bill.

"Naw, you good. Get ya nigga Mason to get you some money to get ya grill fix. Besides, it was his ex-girlfriend new man who fucked ya shit up. You asking your side nigga to preform ya husband duties. All I'm here to do is scratch an itch that your husband has been neglecting. I got my nut and so did you."

"Peanut, you really going to do me like this?"

"I'm going to do you one better. Whatever we have going on is dead. I can't be associated with you or Mason. Especially now I'm making money with Law and Aquil. They have ties to Angelo and the GMM and being associated with y'all is bad for business."

I really needed the money he was about to give me. I can't get hired anywhere with my teeth jacked up. On top of that, I'm twenty-seven years old with no work experience. All I have experience in was stripping and setting niggas up. And right about now, Peanut was looking like a lick.

"Cool, I'll see you around." I grabbed my bag and walked out of his house. If Peanut was smart or truly knew me, he knew I had just threatened him. I saw money in my near future.

Chapter 8

Ira

Today was going to be hard as I walked up to Ms. Ella house. Every year, Ms. Ella throws a cookout on my daughter's mother, Amelia, birthday. Amelia was the love of my life, and she died giving birth to my daughter. Amelia gave the ultimate sacrifice for our daughter. The thing that kills me and will always weigh heavy on my heart is the fact that I wasn't with her when she took her last breath.

It seemed as death always surrounded me. My father, Joseph, died way before my mother could give birth to me. So, the only father figure I had was my Uncle Royal. He treated me like I was his son. Every summer I spent with my Uncle Royal, his wife Aunt Maria, and their kids. But my Uncle and Aunt really stepped up and took on the responsibility of raising me when my mother died of pneumonia when I was fifteen years old.

After my mother died, I was truly lost and acting out. It was plenty of times when my Aunt and Uncle had to beat me and set me straight. I was out here drawling, going back to my old neighborhood, fighting, robbing people, and stealing cars. I didn't have any picks. I was on a road to self-destruction, and it wasn't until my best friend Roscoe was shot in front of me during a robbery gone wrong that things got that bad.

At that moment, I was in one of my deepest depression, mainly, because I pulled Roscoe into that life of crime. I felt like I allowed my inner demons to get my friend killed.

The first time I saw Amelia, I swear I knew she was supposed to be my girl. She was at the house I shared with my Aunt and Uncle and their kids tutoring my Aunt Maria godson, Ricardo. I had just walked in from football practice and I knew Ricardo was just using this tutoring session as a way to bag her. Usually, I would let him be great, but Amelia was too pretty to pass up. I figured Ricardo would just have to take that lost on the chin. He always did this when he liked a girl. He always had females come tutor him over Aunt Maria and Uncle Royal house.

It was like he was trying to showboat more than anything. To him, he wanted females to see his connection to the Black Brothers and maybe they would be truly interested in him. But that always backfired because the girl would always try to get with me or our cousins. It was times females would just act like they were interested in him to get close to one of us.

I sat in the dining room during their whole tutoring session and let Amelia do her thing. I knew she probably thought I was a whole creep by the way I was just staring at her.

As soon as their little session was over, I introduced myself and offered to take her home. Ricardo was pissed that she rather got a ride home than caught the bus with him. That night, we exchanged numbers and became inseparable. Amelia was like a breath of fresh air. She was my new beginning. Slowly but surely, she was bringing me out of my depression. Being with her, it felt like the weight and burden of Roscoe's death and the passing of my mother was being lifted of my shoulders.

After my sixteen birthday, my Uncle started grooming me for the family business. He had already started grooming Pharaoh, Majesty, and King when they turned of age. But he was hesitant when it came to me, mainly because he knew this wasn't the life my mother, his sister, Irene, wanted for her only son. But after my little crime spree after her death, he decided if I was going to live the street life, I should be taught by the people who ran them.

Things were going perfect by the time I graduated high school in 2010, I had enough money to buy me and Amelia matching

2010 Dodge Chargers and was able to keep up on the rent at our new condo in downtown Philadelphia. I had more money than a man twice my age who'd been working their nine-five for twenty plus years. College was never an option for me, but school always had been Amelia's priority. I didn't want my girl to worry about a thing. After we graduated, I took on the responsibility of paying her tuition.

She paid me back by graduating Magna Cum Laude from Penn State University. During her senior year, we found out she was pregnant. We couldn't have been happier; I already knew she was mine so at her graduation party, I proposed to her. Everybody was happy except Ricardo. But he was the least of my worries, so I thought. Finding out that me and my finance were now expecting our daughter, I asked my Uncle and Aunt for more responsibility. I never wanted Amelia and my baby girl to ever want for anything. Plus, if something ever happened to me, I wanted them to still be able to live a comfortable lifestyle.

Red flags had always been popping up. I guess you can say I underestimated people. As the time passed and Amelia pregnancy got further along, I was working hard doing overtime. Every time we had a family event such as Sunday dinners at the Black's household, I would always notice Ricardo staring and trying to throw his little shade my way. I took it as he was jealous because the responsibility Aunt Maria and Uncle Royal was giving me. They barely taught him the ends and outs of the game and honestly, I believed they wasn't going to.

Auntie Maria always said he came off as weak to her. Being as though we were all close, he was present for many business meetings and transactions. Ricardo hated that he had Gonzalez blood running through his body only for me, and outsider with no blood, to get put on.

One day Amelia was coming from the supermarket and ran into Ricardo. She told me through tears that Ricardo gripped her up and shook her violently. She said he was mad and screaming that she was supposed to be his girl and that it was supposed to be his baby growing inside of her. There was nothing left for me to say. I drove right over to his mother, Carla's house and dragged him out the house and beat him damn near to death. The only thing that stopped me was Carla's screams begging me to stop. The look on her face was a look no mother should have had as she witnessed her son's close brush with death.

After that incident, Ricardo kind of disappeared to the background. As for me, I put in more work and fell back from my Uncle and cousins a little. If it wasn't business, I was chilling preparing for my little girl to make her entrance into the world. I just felt it was best; at the end of the day Ricardo was still Aunt Maria's family and godson. I would never put my fiancée in a position to be in the same room as the man who attacked her. So, we kept our distance and they understood.

The night Troi was born was supposed to be the happiest days of our lives, but as life has it was the worst day of my life. I was making one last huge drop before I took some time out and helped my shorty with our daughter. Amelia already expressed multiple times she wanted me to be very active in our daughter's life. For the first two months she wanted me close to home to help. I had no problem with that. She almost killed me because I missed two of prenatal appointments because of business. But, I would be damn if I missed my baby girl's entrance into the world. Amelia's due date wasn't supposed to be until the next week.

The night of the drop, everything was going prefect. Before I left home, I fucked my girl into a comatose sleep. Amelia was always paranoid, and it seemed like ever since that situation with Ricardo, she became even more paranoid. After picking up the drugs, I placed the bricks of heroine inside the secret departments of the car. Things were running smoothly, that was until I was pulled over by the cops. I wasn't worried because the only way they could tell if I had drugs in the car was if an insider had told them. I didn't start to get worried until the canine unit came and they started searching the car. I was heated as they started going straight to the departments where the drugs were hidden.

That's when I knew I was set up and looking at major time. Unbeknownst to me, the same time I was getting arrested, Amelia was going into labor. I was told she had a complicated birth and lost too much blood. She died right there on the operating table. They say it was nothing the doctors could do. I didn't find out about the birth of my daughter and the death of fiancée until I received a visit from my lawyer and Uncle Royal.

I'm not going to even lie to you, a nigga cried. I cried so hard everybody in the jail probably could hear me sobbing. Knowing that she was alone when she died hurt me the most. I would never forgive myself for putting business before her. That night she begged me to stay home. Not only did my fiancée die, but my daughter was left in the world without a mother or a father. I missed four years of my baby girl's life.

Ms. Ella and my Aunt and Uncle really held it down for me while I was locked up. Troi didn't want for anything or miss out on any love. My first year in prison, I was depressed and the only person I talked to was Angelo. That was because he was my cellmate. The only brightness I had in my life was when Ms. Ella would bring Troi to visit me. She never missed a visit and seeing my daughter made me want to pull through. Honestly, it wasn't until my own brush with death that I started to get my shit together. When I got arrested my cousins killed their business partners thinking they was the one who set me up. The police say they receive and anonymous tip. They felt like it had to be the Rodrigues family. Because the only people who knew about the drop was them, and us, and there was no way we would turn on our own.

I honestly always thought Ricardo had something to do with my arrest. He was the only one to gain something from it. With me arrested, he thought that would be his opportunity to gain more responsibility, but that never happened.

One day while me and Angelo was making our way to the

showers, I was attacked by six members of the Rodrigues Crime Family. If it wasn't for Angelo, I would have been dead. The crazy thing was, I barely spoke to him except hi and bye. I was his cell-mate for a full year, and he risked his life for mine. I will always be indebted to him; that's why I ride so hard for Lo, Cream, and GMM. To show my appreciation when he got out, I hooked him up with my cousin Pharaoh. They took GMM to a higher level; within a year's time, GMM has taken over the Tristate.

"Here's my son," Ms. Ella said as soon as I walked in the house. She smiled so bright and as of right now, all I needed was a mother's love. I consider Ms. Ella my second mother ever since Amelia and I started dating. She never looked down on me or treated me different because of my life choices.

"Wassup, ma?" I said, giving her a hug before speaking to every-body else. Her house was full of family and friends, just like every year she throws this cookout.

"Daddy!" Troi screamed, running full speed into my arms. I swear every day she looks more and more like her beautiful mother.

"Hey, lil mama!" I pick her up and threw her in the air. She was six years old now, but she still was going to be my baby girl.

"Daddy, I missed you. I thought you weren't coming."

"I told you he was coming little girl. You know he'll never miss this celebration." Ms. Ella said, tickling Troi.

"Daddy, are you coming from speaking to mommy?" Troi asked. She knew every year on holidays and birthdays I always spend time with Amelia at her gravesite. Every week I place fresh flowers on her grave. I speak to her about everything under the sun. I tell her how much our daughter has grown and how she is just as beautiful and smart as her mother.

"Yes."

"Did you place my card on her tombstone and put the pretty

flowers I picked out in the vase."

"Yes, I did lil mama."

"Cool." She said before running back outside with her cousins.

"How's it going son? How do you feel?" Ms. Ella asked, pulling me to the kitchen table as she started making me a plate.

"Ma, you know how I get around her birthday. All I'm trying to do is chill and smoke a fat blunt for real." I answered honestly.

"I feel you, you brought me my weed right?" She looked at me and all I could do was laugh. Ms. Ella was cool as shit, it was plenty of times we blew complete trees together.

"Yeah, one of my soldiers about to drop some off for you." I said.

"So, you know while I was out shopping we ran into Troi old daycare teacher, Ms. Wilson, and she invited her over." Ms. Ella said waiting on my response.

Ms. Ella think she's slick. Ever since I return home from prison, she been trying to get me back out on the dating scene. Dating has been the last thing on my mind. I felt like nobody could equate to Amelia. The love I have for her will never go away and in all honesty, it'll probably makes my next bitch uncomfortable.

"Oh yeah?"

"Yes. Ms. Wilson was such a big part of Troi's life while you was in prison and she was getting old enough to learn the truth about Amelia. It would really mean a lot to her that she is here. That's why I invited her."

"Okay." I said, shaking my head. I do vaguely remember her telling me about one of Troi teachers in the past.

"But..." She started than gave me a look. I knew she was trying to be match maker.

"I knew there was going to be a but."

"No, Ira. I just want you to be happy again. Listen, no one will ever replace Amelia. But that don't mean put ya life on hold. You're not getting any younger. Troi wants to have a mother figure in her life. She asked me all the time when you going to find her a mommy. I'm getting older. I won't always be here to take care of y'all. Before I go, I need to know that you will be happy." Ms. Ella stressed, looking me dead in the eyes. For some reason, I felt like she was letting me know something was wrong with her.

"Why you talking like you about die?" I asked.

"Cuz, I'm getting old, nigga." Ms. Ella laughed, but I knew she was lying. She was just one of those people who will never tell you her problems because she didn't want to feel like a burden to anyone.

"Alright, mom. You better be taking care of yourself." I said, taking her in and I did notice that she had lost some weight.

"Mama! Daddy! Looks who's here?" Troi said, running into the house, dragging someone behind her.

"Troi, let her go. You have her damn near running after you." Ms. Ella said. "Hey, Ms. Wilson."

"Hi, Ms. Ella." It was the same voice that's been running through my mind ever since the night at the club. Looking up, there was no other than Riley standing in front of us. In the short period of time we chilled with each other at the club she seemed to be cool. We even exchange numbers that night. But shorty definitely curved the shit out of me the next day. After calling her three times with no answer, I left lil mama alone. Plus, she already made it clear that she was in a situation. But judging the rock sitting on her ring finger, shorty was either married or engaged.

"Wassup, Riley." I spoke as I sat there watching the look of surprise cover her face.

"Ira... hey... what are you doing here?"

"Y'all know each other." Ms. Ella asked as she and Troi stood there waiting for an answer.

"Yeah, something like that, Troi's my daughter." I answer both of their questions in one sentence.

"What a small world." Troi said, looking back and forth between me and her former teacher.

Chapter 9

Riley

*D*amn right it's a small world. I thought to myself as the man I have been ignoring and dreaming about is standing here looking me dead in the face. God knew exactly what he was doing when he created Ira Black. This man stood about six feet two inches, skin smooth and dark as Hersey kiss. Just looking at him was causing me to blush. A man hasn't had this effect on me since forever. It was like all I wanted to do was be free and be myself with him. Every day I kicked myself in the ass for ignoring his phone calls. But I knew we could be nothing more than associates because I was engaged to Sebastian Taylor Jr.

"I guess there is no need for introductions since y'all already on first name bases. But this is the godsend teacher and owner of Troi's old daycare." Ms. Ella said, causing me to smile. I love hearing when I make a difference in my children life. I truly love what I do, and teaching children is my passion.

"Come on, Troi, lets go outside." Ms. Ella damn near dragged Troi behind her to give me and Ira some privacy.

"Wassup, stranger? I see your ass been ducking me so much. You fuck around and unbeknownst to you came to my family cookout." He chuckled, showing off his prefect white teeth.

"I wasn't ducking you, Ira." I lied only for him to give me the side eye look.

"Listen, I wanted to reach out to you so bad. But the way my situation is set up. I rather keep my drama to myself."

"Sounds like you need to get out of your situation that you're in." Ira stated. "You're too pretty, and from the way my mother in law and daughter speaks of you, you're good people too. So, you shouldn't be in a situation where you feel trapped." He said. pulling me into his personal space.

All I wanted to do was lean forward and place my lips on his.

"It's easier said than done." I muttered. I can't lie, I felt like shit and a little awkward that I was lusting over this man at his wife's damn memorial cookout.

"Ms. Wilson, come here!" Troi came, inside the house yelling for me.

"Yes, Troi." I answered, following her outside to the backyard, leaving Ira in the kitchen. Outside, Troi took it upon herself to introduce me to everyone. I was surprised to see Reign, Chasity, Tempest, and Queen there, along with their husbands and kids. Even Mama Maria and Royal made an appearance. It was good to see Ira's family also there to support him and Troi on this day.

"Riley Baby," Reign called out to me as they made their way over to me. "What you doing here?"

"Hey y'all," I spoke, giving everybody a hug.

"Troi used to go to my daycare. I saw them at the market and they extended the invitation. So, I came to show my favorite student my support."

"Cousin Tempest, where's Jamie?" Troi asked.

"She's in the house looking for you," Tempest laughed.

"Ms. Wilson, I'll be right back. I want you to meet my cousin and best friend." Troi said, leaving to go search for her friend.

Ira finally made his way outside along with his cousins, Angelo and Cream. I tried everything in my power to keep from staring at him, but I could feel his intense stare trained on me. Which caused me to keep looking in his direction. It was like he was trying to read me or figure out my story.

"So, wassup with you and Ira?" Queen asked.

"Nothing," I looked confused. "Why you ask that?"

"The way y'all are staring at one another has inquiring minds wanting to know if you about to be a part of the Black Family." Chasity answered.

"I met him at the club on his birthday. It was the same day we took Tracey out. I haven't seen or talk to him since." I answered, glancing back in his direction only to find him looking dead at me while he spoke to his people.

"Girl, the way he looking at you got me feeling chills. Mark my words, Ira Black is feeling you. He's giving you the same look Pharaoh gave my ass. Now look at me engage to be married with twins."

"You know I'm engaged, right?" I waved my ring around only for them to turn their nose up, like my engagement ring was Cubic zirconia that Sebastian pick up from a pawn shop. But I looked at all of their rings and quickly put my hand down. My ring ain't have shit on the rocks that were displayed on their fingers.

"Fuck Sebastian's weird ass," Reign hissed. She didn't like him for some reason. Every time I asked why she didn't like him, she would always say she picked up bad vibes from him. The crazy thing is, those vibes are real because Sebastian is everything but the charming man I fell in love with at college.

"Well, just a word of advice. The Black men always get what they want." Mama Maria said, sitting next to me. I didn't even know she was listening to the conversation.

Ms. Ella really did a nice job with this memorial cookout. Everybody had T-shirts made with Amelia face on them. I could tell by the turn out she was truly loved. There was family and friends. Multiple people got up and told their stories about

Amelia and I could tell she touched a lot of people. As people got up to tell their stories Troi started to become sad and after the third person got up, she was in a full blown out cry session. My heart went out to her. I couldn't imagine losing my mother.

Pulling away from her grandmother Troi ran directly pass her father and fell into my arms. I quickly picked her up and took her into the house. This wasn't the first time I had to comfort Troi about her mother. At a young age she had to learn and cope with the loss of her mother and how her mother died.

"Troi, it's going to be okay." I said, rocking her back and forth. We were in the living room by ourselves.

"It's not fair. Everyone have nice stories about her and the only thing I can say is she died having me."

"Baby girl. Your mom wouldn't want you thinking like that. Remember what I told you before." I asked. My heart was breaking for her.

"You said my mom lives through me." Troi said, starting to calm down.

"Yes, she does. Every day she's looking down on you. Look at your shirt." On her shirt was of her mother while she was still pregnant with Troi.

"Look how happy she looks. Look how beautiful she is. You look just like your mother. You are her legacy. Troi, baby, you are the greatest blessing your mother contributed to this world."

"I just miss her."

"I know, baby, but it's going to be okay." I had tears falling from my own eyes. Every girl wants and needs a mother's love.

"You know what would make me feel better." Troi said, looking at me and was surprised I had tears of my own falling.

"What?" I asked as she started to wipe my tears away. "See, Tori, you got me in here crying like a big baby." She laughed showing me her pretty smile.

"What would make me happy is if you and my daddy take me and Jamie to see *The Incredible's 2* at the movies tonight."

"Of course, if it's okay with your dad." I said. There was no way I was telling this girl no.

"It's fine with me," Ira's voice boomed through the room. He was standing in the doorway between the living room and dining room. I had no clue that he was there.

"Yay! Let me tell Jamie." Troi excitedly jumped off my lap and ran in search of her cousin.

"Thank you." Ira said.

"Oh, no problem." I responded quickly as I tried to walk pass him, only for him to grab my arm. Looking in his eyes, it was like he was having a battle with his inner self. Pulling me closer to him, he leaned his tall frame down. His face was so close I knew we was about to kiss.

"Yo, Ira!" Angelo said, walking inside with a plate of food. "Umm, did I interrupt something?"

"Naw." He answered, letting me go.

"Wassup, Riley?" Angelo spoke, giving me a hug.

"Hey, Lo." I spoke before heading back outside.

After spending another hour at the memorial cookout, me and Ira made good on our promise and we took Troi and Jamie to see *The Incredibles 2*. I can admit, I truly had a good time today. It was a first time in a long time I genuinely had fun. I held so many secrets in my life that I needed a break from my reality.

"Did y'all enjoy the movies?" I asked the girl's as we walked out of the movie theatre.

"Yes!" They answered at the same time.

"I think you enjoyed it as much as they did, or more." Ira said with a chuckle.

"So, what I been waiting on the sequel since 2004." I admitted. Shit, I was just happy I had kids to go with me because I was definitely going to be that adult going to see a kid movie. Don't judge me, judge ya boyfriend who's calling his side chick sis.

"I see." Ira said as we grabbed one of the girl's hands as we was about to walk in the parking lot.

As we made our way to the car, something caught my attention. Looking to my right, I saw my fiancée hand and hand with his secretary, Isabella. They looked like they was coming from the direction of the restaurant called, Warm Daddy's. Warm Daddy's was a nice little jazz restaurant in the same shopping plaza as the movie theater. I didn't even know how to feel. His infidelities was nothing new to me. I always spot lipstick on his collar or smell perfume on his clothes while I was doing laundry. But to actually see him with his other bitch had me lost for words. A bitch that always smiled in my face when I was in her presence. I kept my eyes trained on them as I watched them have a mini make out session before walking to the car, which seem to be park directly across from mine and Ira's.

Fuck.

"You okay?" Ira asked as we reached the car.

"Yeah." I answered nervously. There was no way of me escaping Sebastian from seeing me. I couldn't believe I didn't see his car when we parked here. We both helped the girl's get into his truck.

"Is that...." I heard Isabella starting to ask before Sebastian cut her off.

"Come on now." He barked at her, causing me and Ira to look their way. Sebastian's light skin was turning as red as a tomatoes. I knew he was beyond pissed. I didn't know if he was mad that he got caught or he was mad because I was standing talking to Ira

Black.

"I wanted to say thank you again for speaking with Troi. Her not having her mother has been truly hard on her."

"You don't have to thank me. I love Troi and I can't imagine or began to imagine how she feels. So, I will always be here for her. And make sure she's okay. But I want to thank you for allowing me to be a part of y'all day today. I truly enjoyed myself."

"You should let me take you out some time, without the kids." Ira pulled me into his arms, and all I could do was submit to him.

"Sure." Grabbing my chin, he lean down and kissed me soft and passionately. This kiss had my head gone and panties wet that I forgot Sebastian was parked across from us. Reality didn't hit until I heard his tires screeching out of the parking lot.

"Riley, I'm serious. Don't have me out searching for you. Answer the phone when I call." He threatened before kissing me again.

"Whew... okay, I need to get going." I said, forcing myself to push away from him. He reluctantly decided to let me go. But the look on his face looked to be a mixture of disappointment and acceptance.

"Call me when you get to the house," Ira said.

"I will," I said before making my way to my car.

As I unlocked my door, Ira's car window rolled down, and all I could hear was *"Daddy and Ms. Wilson sitting in a tree, K.I.S.S.I.N.G. First comes love, then comes Marriage, then come Ms. Wilson with the baby carriage...."* Embarrassed was an understatement. Here I am, being teased by two six-year-olds.

"Bye girls."

"Bye, Ms. Wilson," they responded before pulling up their windows, still singing the song.

"You hear what I have to drive home listening too?" Ira said, shaking his head.

"You'll be fine." I got in my car and made my way home.

Home was the last place I wanted to be. I was silently praying that Sebastian took himself wherever Isabella lived because this wasn't a fight I wanted to fight. After taking the long way home, I got there within an hour. I didn't see Sebastian's red Benz parked outside, and I breathed a sigh of relief. Unlocking the door, I walked right into Sebastian's fist. Sending me falling onto the floor.

"What the fuck you trying to do Riley? Embarrass me in front of the people I work with?" Sebastian was yelling and kicking me in my stomach.

"Please stop!" I begged.

"Fuck you, hoe." Sebastian grabbing me by my hair and started dragging me up the steps. I knew there was going to be multiple bald spots in my hair after the fight.

"No, fuck you, nigga! I just caught you on a fucking date with ya hoe ass secretary, and you want to come for me." I snapped, getting loose from his grasp. I don't know where this confidence came from, but I knew I fucked up when he punched me dead in my mouth, busting my lips. I started to swing on him, but my punches didn't seem to faze him at all. As a matter fact, all my fighting back did was make him even more angrier.

"You fighting me over this nigga!" It was like he was foaming at the mouth. Picking me up, Sebastian body slammed me on the floor like we was on WWE. I felt the air leaving my body. All I could do was curl into a ball and try to protect myself from his vicious kicks. It felt like the attack had went on for hours. He didn't even stop until he literally couldn't physically attack me anymore.

"Clean ya self-up. If you think about leaving, just know you'll lose everything you worked for." He threatened with his eyes piercing down on me in disgrace.

All I could do was cry. I was back to reality. I felt like I had been run over by a mac truck. The only peace I had was hearing my front door close, letting me know he left. This was his regular M.O after he beat my ass. I won't be seeing him for a couple of days. And when he decides to show his face again, he will be giving me the same *I'm sorry lies.*

"Why God…. this can't be life." I cried down on my cherry wood floor in my bedroom.

Chapter 10

Tracey

I've been home for a couple of weeks now, and my transition back to society has been nothing but great. My parole officer, Officer Tate, is cool. When I first went to see her, I was expecting some old lady or white man who would be looking down on me for my past choices. But to my total surprise, she was a young African American woman who just wants to see her parolees stay on a good path. I'm working in Reign's spa which always keeps me busy. I'm able to pay all of my bills. Even though Angelo said, he got me I didn't want to take advantage of his kindness. I'm twenty-three years old, and I needed to learn to take care of myself. I didn't want to come out of jail depending on him or anyone for that matter. My life seemed great the only thing missing is reuniting back with my parents

God knows I miss Tanya and Thomas Harris. My parents were God send and looking back I couldn't believe how I took them for granted. Only thing I can think of is love can make you do some crazy things. Not speaking to my parents in five years honestly broke my heart. After I accepted the plea deal, I tried countless times to reach out to them, but they would never accept the charges for my phone calls. It was times like when I went through my miscarriage that I needed my mother's support. Especially, since she had a couple miscarriages herself before they had me. I knew my mother was probably one of the only people I could vent too about that tragic experience. The only thing that kept going through my mind was the last words I ever spoke to them.

Fuck y'all I don't need you!

At the age of eighteen, I thought I knew everything. I knew Mason had my back and our love would prosper. Only for him to prove everybody right. That was a hard pill to swallow. I literally turned my life upside down. It's crazy because even though my parents didn't support my choices according to Reign, they still looked out by putting money on my books. Pulling up to my parent's house I got butterflies in my stomach. I was so nervous that I sat in the car for about ten minutes contemplating whether I should ring the doorbell. Sucking up my fear of rejection I made my way to my parent's front door.

"I been wondering when you was going to get out of your car." My mother said opening the door before I could ring the doorbell.

"Mom." Was all I could get out before I fell into her arms and sobbed uncontrollably. Tanya wrapped her arms around me in only a way a mother could.

"It's okay baby girl. Come on in." She said as we walked inside the house my father had built up from the ground for us. Looking around everything still looked the same. They still have pictures of me and Reign align around the walls.

"I'm sorry." I apologized as soon as we sat down in the living room.

"I know baby. Tracey, you always been a stubborn child. Your stubbornness is a trait your father passed along to you. You always been a child that had to live and learn. It's just sad that this was a lesson you had to learn the hard way." My mom said, and I couldn't deny it.

"Mom that was the worst experience of my life."

"I bet." She got up and walked over to the bar and grabbed two glasses and a bottle of wine.

"I feel so stupid. While I was in prison, I found out I was pregnant." My mother gasped at my omission.

"I cried every day I didn't want to have a baby in jail. But I knew my baby deserved a chance to live."

"Where's my grandchild?" my mother asked.

"Please don't tell you allowed him to become a ward of the state."

"No, I lost him. I miscarried." I answered feeling myself losing the battle to keep my tears at bay.

"Oh, Tracey." She placed her wine glass down and sat next to me on the sofa,

"I'm sorry you had to go through that alone."

"I blame myself every day for my miscarriage."

"Baby you can't go through life blaming yourself. Sometimes tragic situations are all about God's plan to make you stronger."

"No mom my baby died because I stop taking care of myself. I wasn't eating. I was basically starving myself. How could I be so selfish." I cried.

"Tracey, why would you do that? Did something happen while you were in jail." I could tell my mom was beginning to panic.

"No" I sighed.

"During one of my visits. Mason came to visit me. I told him that I was pregnant. The man that I loved looked me straight in the eyes and told me he didn't want the baby we created together. Like he had an option." The anger was building up inside of me once again as I spoke about my unborn. Me losing my baby will always be an open wound that will never heal.

"I swear I never hated someone until I laid eyes on Mason. He always came off as sneaky. And what was worst it was like he had you wrapped around his finger. What type of man can't man up and raise his child after allowing his girlfriend to go to jail for him?!"

"That's not even the worse part. After that visit Mason stop visiting me, writing letters, and of course, the money stopped. Mason straight up abandoned me. Reign already gave me her word that she will raise my child until I got out of jail. The information that pushed me over the edge was his wife?"

"Wife!" My mom shouted pouring herself another drink.

"Yes, wife. It was some girl that I always thought they was messing around. But she confirmed my suspicion when she sent me a letter explaining their involvement with one another. Along with a maternity picture, her ultrasound, and wedding announcement."

"That bitch."

"I can't even lie to you. I was broken. So, broken that I tried to commit suicide. I lost everything because of Mason."

"Tracey Lynn." My mom gasped holding her chest. It wasn't long before her waterworks started.

"'m sorry I wasn't there to help you through this."

"Mom stop apologizing. It's not your fault that you wasn't there." The last thing I wanted was for my mother to feel any type of guilt. Especially, when I pushed her and my father away.

"Listen sometimes God places you in certain situation to open our eyes. You definitely needed an eye opener when it came to Mason."

"Your right. Mom, I just want to say sorry again. I can never stop telling you and daddy how sorry I am."

"Tracey it's okay. I'm just happy you came to see me. Reign let me know when you got out and honestly, I was hurt that you didn't come sooner. But I do want to say I'm sorry. As a mother, I should have never turned my back on you. As a mother, I should have been the bigger person."

"Babe I'm home who's G Wagon parked outside of our house. I know that boy Pharaoh didn't buy Reign another car." I heard his chuckle as he made his way to the Livingroom. My nerves was on overdrive not knowing what his reaction was going to be.

"What's going on here?" My father Thomas voice boom through the room causing me and my mom to jump.

"Hey, Honey Tracey, stop by to speak with us." I could hear the uneasiness in her voice.

"Hi dad" I spoke walking up to him only for him to look down at me with disgust.

"Tracey." He spat my name like it left a bitter taste in his mouth." Tanya escort your guest out my house. She's no longer welcome here.

"Thomas," my mom hissed. Looking back and forth between me and my father. My heart was broken. Before Mason, I was a true daddy's girl. I could do no wrong in my father eyes.

"She is always welcome here."

"No, the fuck she's not," he barked.

"She made her decision when her dumb ass was out here ruining her life and ours!"

"Daddy I'm sorry... I'm just going to go." I muttered rushing pass him and out of the house, I once called home. Thomas Harris never spoke to me in that manner ever in my life. I knew it wasn't going to be easy getting back into my parent's good graces. But for him to treat me like I wasn't his daughter, or there was no love left in his heart for me. Was truly killing me softly.

"Tracey!" I heard my mom calling my name from behind.

"Mom I'll call you later." I quickly said not stopping my stride towards my car.

"Tracey you have to forgive your father and just give him some time. When you went to jail that didn't just affect your life. Your father's career has suffered in ways you can't imagine. Thomas work hard to achieve his goals and knock down every roadblock that came his way. During the time you were going through your legal battle he was up for a promotion and for Chief of Surgery. With this promotion not only would he be the head of all of the surgeons in the hospital he would be the face of the department. Long story short his connection with you made them overlook him for the promotion and give it to a doctor he trained as a resident who is less qualified. That was a blow to his ego that he was willing to take, but he felt like everything was in view. When you took that plea deal. It was a smack in the face.

"Tell him I'm sorry," I said to my mom before hopping in my car and pulling off. The whole drive home I cried tears of regret and hurt. Thinking about my past choices made my hate for Mason grow even more. But the reality of my life is that I can blame him all I want. The truth is I made the decision that caused a ripple effect of negativity in everybody's life.

Chapter 11

Naomi

"You don't have to go home, but you have to get fuck out of here." I joked with my sister Lala; we currently chilling at my house having drinks. But my babe was on his way over, and I needed shorty to roll out.

"You always kicking somebody out for Angelo."

"Don't be jealous sissy. I've been working all week, and I need some quality time with my man." I said.

"Ya man? I didn't know you guys were official." Lala said giving me the side eye.

"We're not official, official. You can say we're serious. He's the only on that I'm talking to. You know he's not all into titles. We let shit flow. But I've been talking to him for about three years now. It doesn't get any more serious than that." I said hoping I didn't sound as stupid as the look on my sister's face.

"Naomi during those three years he been out here fucking other bitches, sis." Lala rolled her eyes. She hated the situation me and Angelo called ourselves having. And she never let a minute go by without letting me know how she truly feels.

"Well, what we have is not for others to understand."

"Bitch I don't think you understand what y'all have. Naomi, you deserve so much better than what you're willing to accept. You claiming a man that will never claim you. He only comes over when he's ready to use you to bust his nut and dip when he's done. The nigga doesn't even spend the night when y'all done. Seriously, you a gorgeous woman and look at you putting all this effort in this night y'all supposed to have together. Dinner on the stove; dining table set for the perfect romantic dinner fit for a King...."

"Get out hoe!" I snapped cutting her off. I was annoyed by the truth she just expressed.

"Don't get mad at me for spitting straight facts."

"You're still here."

"Don't call me pissed and wanting to vent after he walk his black ass up in here and don't eat your food and leave right after he blow your back out. I don't want to hear it because all I'm going to do is tell you I told you so."

"Whatever," I muttered as I watch her grab her purse and make her way to the door.

"Bye Naomi. Call me later, but not about Angelo. Love you."

"I won't be calling you until Monday because tonight is Friday and Angelo will be staying all weekend."

"Right," Lala stated sarcastically before heading to her car.

"Bye Lala enjoy spending time with your new step-son." I knew I just hit her below the belt, but she was getting on my damn nerves.

"Fuck you!"

"Love you too sis," I said and quickly shut my door before her crazy ass ran back up my steps and tried to fight me.

I hated when Lala always tried to point out my faults in my relationship with Angelo. Especially, when she can barely keep her own marriage on track. Just a couple month ago she found out that her husband Samuel was having an affair for the last two years. That affair resulted in a baby, and now the woman is taking not only Samuel for child support but Lala too. Ain't that a bitch? Some people may think I'm crazy for standing by Angelo and putting my all to what we're trying to build. But the heart wants what the heart wants. I can't front and act like our secrecy's don't bother me; but when we first started dealing with each other hiding, our relationship was always in my best interest.

I met Angelo three years ago when he was released from jail. He was one of my new parolees. The day he walked in my office, and his cologne invaded my nostrils I knew I was in trouble. Standing 6'3, caramel skin tattoos covered his arms and neck. God I was willing to throw my whole career away to hop on him and do some ungodly acts. Angelo was so smooth he had a way of making you go against the grain to satisfy him. Two months of being his parole officer things was running smoothly and me not being distracted by his handsome face. Things took a turn one night; I was out with some of my college friends, and we were attending the grand opening at *Club Royal.*

Long story short I was gone off the Henny and didn't have the strength to reject him. That night Angelo ended up at my house, and I ended up face down ass up as he fucked the shit out of me from the back. My neighbors definitely knew his name that night. Angelo fucked me so good that night, I woke up the next morning ready to cook him breakfast.

Only to find that he was no longer at my house. I didn't hear him leave; it was like he was the pussy bandit or a thief in the night. I had to walk around my house to make sure he didn't rob my dumb ass blind. I couldn't believe I slipped up this bad. Not only did I sleep with a felon I slept with one who I was supposed to be paroling. Everything was in jeopardy. Going back to work I was on pins and needles. Especially, since I was going to see Mr. Angelo Hart bright and early.

That morning he came into my office with his famous smirk. I knew this visit would be interesting. My plan was to go on and act like that night never happened. I was going to do my job and get our meeting over with as soon as possible. However, Angelo had other things on his mind that day.

"Good morning Mr. Hart you can shut the door and have a seat, and we can get you in and out of here today," I said as I watched him walking into my office and shut the door. His eyes bore into me as I tried not to cower under his stare.

"I'm Mr. Hart? Last week I was Daddy." He said sitting down in front of me showing me those perfect white teeth.

"Mr. Hart let's just stay professional."

"Too late for that Officer Sanchez," He said standing up and walking around the table and pulling my chair out so I could face him.

"Ummm mmm" I cleared my throat.

"I need you to take your drug test. Here is the cup go to the bathroom. I'll have Officer Derrick Richards escort you."

"I'll do that in a few. Right now, I think I need to remind you of last Friday. I don't like the fact that you trying to act like what happen at your house never happened."

"What?!" I muttered with my eyes opened as wide as they could go. I know he was not trying to do what I think he was trying to do.

"Listen you're my Parole Officer, and I'm going to let you do ya job. But take care of daddy first."

I don't know what it was, but it was like he had a spell on me. Everything about him was alluring. I am at my job; I couldn't believe I was about to take it there with him with my coworkers and boss on the other side of my door. Unbuckling his belt, he let his pants drop I moved forward with pulling out the tool that brought me to multiple orgasms.

"Stand up," Angelo demanded in a hush tone. It felt like a volcano erupted within me down below. Following his command, I stood in front of him. My breath became short as I waited with anticipation as to what this man was going to do next. Picking me up he placed me on my desk knocking whatever was in his way off the desk.

"Angelo..." I mumble starting to have second thoughts. Was I truly going to put my job and more in jeopardy? Before I could protest Angelo lifted up my skirt to the suit up and quickly snatched my panties off.

"We can't do this.... Not here."

"Shut up," Angelo muttered before ramming his dick inside me causing me to moan out. This man and his long dick was all I've been fantasizing about. Now I finally have it. To keep from screaming out loud, I bit down on his shoulder. He didn't seem to mind as he continued to long stroke me.

"Fuck!"

"Who pussy is this?" Angelo whispered in my ear, and it was like my pussy had a mind of his own. In response she released a gut-wrenching orgasm that had my legs shaking uncontrollably.

"Yours!"

The sound of my phone ringing pulled me out of my little daydream. Let's just say that was the first and definitely not last time Angelo had his way with me in my office. But I want more; there was no reason to hide our relationship anymore. My goal is to let him know that I'm ready to take the next step.

"Hello."

"I'm on my way. Be ass naked by the time I get there." Angelo's voice came through the phone. See I spoke him up.

"Okay, daddy," I answered before he hung up. Tonight is going to be one hell of the night. My pussy muscles already throb in anticipation of what he was about to make my body experience.

Chapter 12

Angelo

Lighting up my blunt I drove to Naomi's house. After the day I had all I wanted to do was slide up inside some good pussy before heading home. Today was my weekend to visit the big homie Blue. Me and Cream alternated weekends visiting him. Even though Blue is serving a life sentence, we still gave him updates on what's going on, on the outside world. Plus, Blue is running a whole drug ring in his prison. Today's visit was a little different mainly because I came to speak to him about Mason.

Honestly, I just wanted to kill Mason he been a liability to GMM. I respect Blue's opinion. He always been the cool level headed one out of him and Sean. But Blue's loyalty to Mike always seem to be my biggest roadblock. Blue and Mike are both active members of GMM. I'm the leader because of who my brother is plus I was the one who actually put GMM on the map. It wasn't much Blue could do on the inside, so he had no problem passing the throne down to me, Cream, and Ira.

Mike is Blue's right-hand man and help's run his little operation in jail. Mike knew Mason was no longer apart of GMM, and knew he needed to keep Mason on a short leash. He knew Mason consequences should have been far worse than him getting jumped out of GMM for what he did to Tracey and the side business that he was doing with the undercover cops. Mike pleaded for Mason's life with Blue and Sean, and they oblige.

Now Blue was asking me not to kill him. He felt like Mason's bloodshed would cause too many problems in the inner circle.

Me killing Mason will make Blue eventually kill Mike. Mike knew too much of his operation, and he knew with Mason's death Mike would probably do anything to avenge his brother. I felt like Mike knew the rules to the game and was taking his friendship with Blue and Sean for granted. If anyone else did what Mason had done a bullet would have been pierce his skull.

Blue already knew I wasn't going to let Mason get away with claiming GMM without any consequences. So, he simply told me to teach him a lesson but don't kill him and he'll talk to Mike. Pulling up to Naomi's driveway I put out my blunt. Naomi was a shorty I been messing with for the past three years. She was my parole officer turned fuck buddy. I like our situation because all we use each other for is sex. I didn't have to worry about her catching feelings because we could never be together. Our little arrangement is about to come to an end now Tracey is home.

When Tracey first came home, I wanted to pick up where we left off before I went to jail. I felt like Tracey needed some time to get herself together before we try to created anything. Tracey jumped from relationship to relationship only for her to get hurt in the end. I needed her to get herself together and let go of that hurt. I'm not going to be punished for the last niggas mistakes. Seeing the way she reacted at the club told me that she wasn't ready for what I had to offer. Ringing Naomi's doorbell, I waited patiently for her to open the door.

"Angelo," Naomi answered the door in some booty shorts and sports bra.

"I thought I told you to be ass naked when I pulled up," I said pulling her towards me and kissing her on her neck.

"I know," she let out a subtle moan before pulling away from my grasp.

"I wanted to do something different."

"What is this?" I inquired as I followed her into the dining room. Shorty had the lights dimmed, and candles lit. The soft melodies of Sade playing in the background. With a full course meal spread across the dining room table.

"This is what I wanted to do different. I wanted to cook you dinner. We never spend quality time together."

Looking at Naomi, I shook my head in disappointment. I thought we had an understanding on what we head going on. That's the main reason why she was still around.

"Why you look so upset? You don't like the food that I cooked."

As good as that food looks and smell I wasn't eating that shit. There are certain things that I won't do when it comes to the woman who I use as fuck buddies. I never wanted them to feel like they could be more than what I expected them to be. I thought I've been doing a good job of not giving them the wrong impression. I keep everything very simple and follow my own personal rules. If I'm not serious with you I don't kiss you on the lips, eat pussy, I don't eat any home cooked meals, and I damn sure don't spend the night. So, to see Naomi go through all this trouble to set up this romantic meal threw me for a loop.

"I didn't come over here to eat. I came to bust a nut."

"Do you have to be so blunt? I have so much more to offer you besides my pussy Angelo."

"Naomi, what are you talking about? I don't want shit else you have to offer. I like our little arrangement. Why are you trying to change it?"

"I don't like our arrangement anymore. I want more. We've been talking for about three years. I knew being together, in the beginning, was a risk, and we had to keep what we were building on the down low because I was your parole officer. But now you're no longer on parole we can be out in the open about our relationship."

What relationship? This bitch is delusional.

"Angelo..." Naomi continued but got cut off by the ringing of my phone.

"Yo." it was Tracey. I haven't seen her in a week, and all we been doing was texting here and there.

"I want to see you."

"You good," I asked because I didn't like the way she sounded. I knew she was supposed to see her parent's today.

"I will be as soon as you get here. So, are you coming?"

"Yeah, Tracey I'm coming. You cook?" I was high as hell and had the munchies like a muthafucka.

"Yeah now come on. I miss you." She moaned, and my dick bricked up without hesitation.

"Alright, I'm on my way make me a plate." Totally forgetting that Naomi went out her way to make me dinner.

"Okay," Tracey responded before hanging up.

"Are you serious!" Naomi shouted walking into my personal space.

"First you answer your phone like we weren't in the middle of talking. And Tracey I hope that's not the bitch who's name you have tatted on your chest."

"Watch ya mouth." I forgot when we first started talking she inquired about the person who name I got tatted. All I told her was she was the one who got away. The day I got Tracey's name tatted it was on some random shit. I took her to get her first tat done; my homie Quadir had just opened up his shop. When she was done, I surprised her and got her name tatted. During this time in our relationship, Tracey had already expressed her feelings. Being as though I truly felt the same and was in love with her. I never voiced it; instead I showed her what I couldn't say.

"Angelo..." She started. I can't lie the look on Naomi face tugged at a nigga's heart a little. Even though Naomi was nothing but my fuck buddy, she was cool people. Shorty really looked out while I was on parole and maybe if Tracey wasn't in the picture, I would seek more out of our situation.

"Naomi, I don't know how I gave you the impression that I wanted to be more than just friends with benefits. I apologize for misleading you. I'm just going to head out."

"What? Wait... you don't have to leave I'm tripping. I knew what this was just forget that I did this. Let's go upstairs." She grabbed my hand only for me to pull away.

"Naw I'm good love come lock up," I said before making my way out her front door. I guess that's a wrap. There was no way I could start back dealing with her. I already seen first-hand how females lose their damn mind over a nigga. If you read Allie Marie's story about my sis Reign, you seen how crazy that bitch Bria was over the homie Pharaoh. I'm not trying to have those problems is my life. Pulling out of Naomi's driveway I made my way across town to Tracey house. When I pulled up all of her lights was out.

"I'm outside," I said as soon as she answered the phone.

"Use the key I know you have to let yourself in." Tracey smart ass said. All I could do was chuckle. I never used my keys to her house because I never wanted her to feel like I was overstepping my boundaries. But yeah, I had a key to the house I paid the rent out in full.

"If this type of treatment I'm getting I could have stayed where I was," I said as I walked to her from door and unlocked it. I stop dead in my tracks as I watched her walk down the steps in nothing, but a black lace bra and thong set. Her hair was down her back with spiral curls.

"The treatment your about to receive you're not going to get anywhere else." She finally reached me and smile grabbing my hand as she lead me up the steps. We went straight to the bedroom. Once inside her bedroom, she directed me into her personal bathroom which had a Jacuzzi and a walk-in shower. Inside the lights was dimmed, and candles was lit all around the Jacuzzi which was already filled and had red and yellow rose peddles floating in the water just awaiting our bodies.

"So, you know I went to see my parents today." She said out of the blue as I kicked off my shoes and she started to undress me.

"Yeah, so what happened?"

"Me and my mom made up. It was like she was waiting for me to show my face. It's crazy I didn't know how much I missed her until I laid eyes on her. I guess me trying to survive while in prison I kind of kept my parents to the back of my mind. Especially since I knew how much my decision disappointed them."

"Your dad?" I asked. I already knew Tracey's mom Tanya was going to welcome her with open arms. Tanya has been putting money on Tracey's books since she was locked up. She even pulled up on me a couple times to get updates about Tracey's wellbeing.

"Let's just say he wasn't as thrilled to be in my presence. Long story short he told me to get the fuck out of his house." She said as we both sat down in the Jacuzzi and allow the jets to massage our body.

"He told you to get the fuck out?" I asked for clarification, so I knew what I was checking her daddy about before I run in his mouth for disrespecting her.

"Yeah don't worry about it. I guess I deserved it in a way. I don't know why I would think he would be ready to welcome me with open arms."

"The disrespect was not warranted. At the end of the day, you made a decision as an adult. Regardless if everybody thinks your decision was poorly made. You made and stood by it and took the bid. Five years later if he can't get over it then fuck it. But there's no reason to be disrespectful and keep punishing you for the choices you made in the past." I said.

"You're right. His reaction just caught me by surprise. My dad never talked to me in that manner before. But enough about him." She stood up and straddled me facing me."

"Why you playing?" I muttered my dick was on brick and at her opening.

"I'm not playing. I want you in the worse way possible and ya ass been too busy." She said kissing me on lips.

"I was just giving you some time to readjust and figure out what you needed. I didn't want you to think because I set you up nice, and made sure you was good that you had to throw the pussy at me." I answered honestly.

"Lo..." she moans rubbing the tip of my dick on her swollen clit.

"Tracey are you sure about this?" I asked one last time. I needed to know. Because once we cross this line, there was no turning back. I was beyond possessive of what I consider mine.

"Yes, Lo I'm ready. I've been waiting on this for years. The way my life is right now; I all I need is you." She said looking me in the eyes as I position her right where I needed her to be.

"You know once I slide up in here its mine. Don't be the reason why somebody mama wearing a black dress." I threatened kissing the side of neck.

"Very romantic." She chuckled.

"Tracey..."

"I know Angelo you're serious. Just know the same goes for you. I better be the only one you're dealing with no bullshit."

I nodded before I focused my attention on her body. Everything about Tracey was beautiful. In my eyes, she was perfect her dark brown skin was blemish free. Her breast was full, stomach flat and her ass was just enough; it wasn't too big or too small. I was enough to grab, and it was the finishing asset to her perfect hourglass shape. I was Tracey first, but tonight was the night that I was going to relearn her body. I wanted to know what turned her on. What spots I needed to kiss to cause for her to submit to me? How many strokes would it take her to cum? What's her favorite position? A nigga needed to know everything. Starting with her lips, I kissed them passionately before moving down to her neck marking my territory. Soft moans escaped her lips as I paid close attention the too breast taking in one nipple at a time.

"Stand up," I demanded, and she did as she was told. Placing one of her legs over my shoulders. I came face to face with the prettiest pussy I ever laid eyes on. It was smooth and freshly waxed, and her natural smell was hypnotizing me. Diving in head first tasting everything she had to offer. Little did she know I've been waiting for this moment myself? A nigga like me loved eating pussy; I just wasn't one to eat everybody's pussy.

"Angelo." She moaned my name as she grabbed on to my shoulders for dear life.

"You taste good." I moaned snaking my tongue all around her pussy. The more I tasted her, the harder my dick got with anticipation of sliding into her sugar walls.

"Fuck.... I'm cumming." Tracey juices started to pour from her pussy into my mouth as her body shook. Allowing her to come down from her orgasmic high, I pull her down to straddle me."

"Damn." I groaned as I slid her down on my rod. Tracey was so tight if I didn't pop her cherry, I would have thought she was a virgin. I had to take my time and allow her to adjust to my width and length.

"Shit... I can fill you in my stomach." She muttered as she started to rock her hips back and forth allowing me more access. Gripping her hips I quickly I slide the rest of me inside of her.

"Ahhhh!" She screamed as her nails dug in my back.

"You okay," I asked kissing her face.

"Mmmm hmmm." Planting her feet on the floor of the Jacuzzi she started to bounce up and down. She didn't even care that she was getting the floor wet.

"Fuck Tracey" I muttered trying to control her movements. Tracey was riding the shit out of me and the way her pussy muscle was gripping my dick I was on the verge of making her a mother.

"Tracey slow down you about to make me cum."

"Cum with me daddy." She said the magic words grinding harder on me. It was only seconds later we both were cumming, and I was straight shooting up the club. I wasn't sure if she on birth control, but after that nut I just bust it's probably too late to get on it.

"Get up I need to redeem myself. You had me cumming quicker than a virgin boy getting pussy for the first time." I said shaking my head. I was low key disappointed in myself.

"I still came." Tracey chuckled.

I didn't even reply to her as I got out of the jacuzzi and she followed suit. Picking her he up she wrapped her legs around my waist, and I made our way to the bed. Laying her down I started kissing her neck and made a trail moving to her breast. Tracey's nipples were hard and pointed right at me ready for me to take them into my mouth. While sucking and kissing on her breast I allowed my digits to explore her passion. She was dripping wet ready for what I had to offer her. Placing both legs on my shoulder, I slid inch by inch into moist tunnel.

"Oh....my ...God" Tracey moaned as I deep stroked her middle, making sure I was hit her g-spot with everyone. I continued to hit her spot until she let out a gut-wrenching scream as her body shook and she started squirting everywhere

"Damn baby you wetting me up." I kissed her on her face as I allowed her legs to drop."

"Turn over," I slapped her on ass.

Tracey did as I demanded with her chest flat on the bed and ass in the air; creating a massive arch in her back. Sliding back into her sugar walls Tracey started to throw that ass back meeting my every stroke. Grabbing a fist full of her hair I pulled her back and landed a sloppy passionate kiss on her lips. Not missing a beat. The visual in front of me would've had me on the verge of busting the biggest nut ever.

"Fuck..." I groaned as we came together again for her fourth time and my second. Laying on the bed, we both tried to normalize our breathing pattern. Her pussy was so good a nigga ws on his way to sleep.

"No daddy I'm not done," Tracey said massaging my dick bringing it back to life.

"What you about to do with him?" I asked lazily. She never answered as she put my dick in her mouth and started to deep throat him like a fucking champ. Yeah, Tracey was stuck with me and if she thought about leaving it's only going to be through a body bag.

∞∞∞

Lying in bed after going several rounds with Tracey she lay sleep in my arms. The disrespect her dad brought her way was bothering me. Mr. Thomas always been cool back in the day, but I've never been one to be tolerant of disrespect. Looking at my watch it was six in the morning. I pulled from underneath her.

"Where are you going?" Tracey asked halfway sleep.

"I'm about to get us some breakfast," I answered. A nigga was hungrier than a muthafucka. I was so busying fucking and eating pussy all night long I didn't even eat the meal she made me.

"It's too early come back to bed." she whined.

"Tracey I'll be right back."

"It's food downstairs."

"I don't want dinner food for breakfast. Go back to sleep. I'm going to get the food, and after we eat, I'm sliding right back in you." I slapped her on her bare ass causing her yell out.

I hopped in the shower and got dressed and headed out the front door. I was making a little detour. It took me twenty minutes to get to Tracey parents' house. I knew both Mr. Thomas and Ms. Tanya was home because their cars was parked in the driveway. Getting out the car I picked the locked to their front door. *They still too comfortable these niggas still ain't get an alarm system*

The house was dark as I made my way upstairs. I guess they decided to sleep in this morning. Walking into their bedroom, Mr. Thomas was laid asleep on the chaise lounge looking very uncomfortable, and Ms. Tanya was on their bed. There was a note on the dresser telling Mr. Thomas not to sleep in her bed.

"Wake up," I demanded tapping Mr. Thomas in the head with my gun. I wasn't going to shoot him. I just didn't want him to jump bad, and I have to beat Tracey's dad up.

"What the hell?" Mr. Thomas jumped up with panic written all over his face.

"Oh my god!" Ms. Tanya screamed as she woke up from Mr. Thomas outburst.

"Angelo?"

"Good morning," I spoke like I didn't just break into their house.

"Let's go for a ride," I told Mr. Thomas who looked like he

wanted to throw hands. I know the only thing that stopped him was because I had my gun in my hands which was by my side.

"Boy did you just break into my house." Mr. Thomas asked.

"Naw I just let myself in. I'm here because I heard you were disrespectful to Tracey. You know I always had respect for y'all but coming for her is a huge NO. Shorty felt some kind of way the way you kicked her out your house."

"Are you serious?" Mr. Thomas said in disbelief.

"Thomas, I told you, you were too harsh. Is Tracey okay." Ms. Tanya said getting out of bed in her silk pajama short set. I couldn't even deny Ms. Tanya had it going on I just hope Tracey was blessed with her genes.

"Tanya get ya ass in bed" Mr. Thomas demanded.

"Showing this nutcase what belongs to me."

"She cool. Mr. Thomas get up we're going for a ride." I said losing my patience.

"I ain't going anywhere with you."

That was it I gripped Mr. Thomas up by his arm like I was a mother in Walmart about beat her son ass for having a tantrum.

"I'm not going to ask again?"

"Angelo, where are you taking him?" I could see the fear in Ms. Tanya's face. My reputation precedes me and my name. They know how I got down as a youngbul they could only imagine. I'm even more ruthless now as an adult.

"He'll be back, he's coming with me to say sorry to Tracey."

"Thomas just go with him. I don't know why you want to try this boy. He obviously doesn't have nothing to lose; he broke into our in broad daylight." Ms. Tanya stressed to her husband. Mr. Thomas groaned as he started to get up and get dressed. Once dress I escorted him to my car. Ms. Tanya got in hers and followed us the whole time.

"Why are we here?" Mr. Thomas asked as I stopped at Angie's Soul Food a restaurant around the corner from Tracey's house to get our breakfast.

"Come on you buying me and my girl breakfast, had me wasting all this damn time to get you out of your house." He didn't even say shit just handed me over a fifty-dollar bill.

"Thanks." I went and picked up the food and continued to Tracey's house.

"Let's get this over with." Mr. Thomas muttered.

"Listen when we walk up in her house speak and show her some respect. When you say, your apology make sure it sounds sincere. Mr. Thomas I would hate to break ya fucking hands for playing with me. I know your hands are how you make your living being a brain surgeon and everything. Do we have an understanding?"

"Understood." He hissed. He could be mad all he wanted; fuck around he'll be putting in for early retirement.

"Babe, what the hell took you so long? I was about to make my own breakfast...." Tracey yelled walking from the kitchen but stopped short when she saw her father standing in her living room.

"What's going on?"

"Ya father has something to say to you. I said sitting at the dining room table about to dig in my food.

"Thomas do what you came here to do. You don't want to keep ya wife waiting."

"Tracey... you sure know how to pick them." He started causing me to jump up. I see he wants to play fucking games.

"Is this what you came here for?" Tracey asked walking up to him with her hands on her hips.

"No, I had a surprise visit today from your little friend," Thomas said tilting his head at me.

"Anyway, I'm here now. Tracey, I want to apologize to you. I should have never spoken to you the way that I did. It was uncalled for and rude. Tracey, I will forgive you one day, but as of now I need time."

"Five years ain't enough." She asked, and I could tell she was hurt.

"I have to come to terms with a lot of things. All I asked is for some time. I promise I'll come around Sweet pea. Just give me some time."

"Okay." She nodded. All she could do was respect that man wishes and all I asked of him is to never disrespect her again.

"You can let ya self out," I said causing Tracey to shake her hand at me.

"Angelo what did you do?" She asked as soon as the front door shut.

"I had a little chat with your father. I don't care how he may feel. But he should never disrespect you the way he did. What I need you to do is respect his wishes and give him time. You going to jail changed everybody. I don't know how it personally affected him but give that man his time."

"I will," she chuckled smiling.

"What?"

"You're really crazy. I'm not even going to ask about the details of how you got him to come over here. But thank you, I needed to hear his apology."

"I know a way you can thank me," I smiled.

"I got you as soon as I'm done eating." She smirked seductively.

Yeah, I'm about hit Reign up and let her know Tracey going to be out for a couple of days.

Chapter 13

Riley

Today is my first day back to work. I've been recovering from the beat down that Sebastian gave me for the past week. Of course, I haven't seen or heard from him all week and to be honest, I was happy. After driving myself to the hospital, I found out I had two fractured ribs and my busted lip and black-eyed had healed a little I was still caking my face up with makeup to cover the bruises. I want to walk away from Sebastian so bad but everything that I work hard for falls into his hands.

Sebastian asked me to marry him the day of my graduation. In the beginning, he wasn't this abusive, manipulative, hateful man he is now. He was sweet and genuine and truly cared about me. I always told Sebastian my dreams and goals was to own a chain of daycares throughout inner-city Philadelphia. I wanted to have affordable daycare for the family that lives in the city of Philadelphia. Philadelphia didn't have daycares and programs that helped parents who had low income? However, I wanted to cater to everyone especially the parent who income wasn't high, but it was too high to be considered for CCIS or other financial assistance programs that helped with childcare.

Sebastian loved my idea and decided to invest in it. His family was very wealthy and respectful throughout the community. Being as though we were getting married, I allowed him to put the business in his name. Especially since he was backing everything financial. Now I have five daycares under my belt, and truly none of them belong to me. Even though it was my blood, sweat, and tears that built the businesses from ground up. Not only does he have control over my businesses he owns the house that I live in and the car that I drive. I don't even know how I got to this place. I guess you can say I was young and dumb and believe that me and Sebastian would be forever. I never saw the signs that he was abusive until he punched me in the face the first time. Opening the bottle of Percocet that my doctor prescribe I popped two. I was still in terrible pain.

"Riley you have this fine ass gentleman asking to speak with you at the front desk."

"Did you ask him his name, Kim." I shook my head. Kim was my service coordinator at my daycare, and she was always checking out the kid's fathers. I had to almost break up a fight due to her obnoxious flirting. If she wasn't good at her job and wasn't Sebastian's little cousin, I probably would have been fired her.

"You know I did girl he said his name is Ira Black. I know you didn't want to be bothered, but he was adamant on speaking to you. I never seen him before. I was trying to get all of his information. I even handed him an application to the daycare. One for employment and one for his child to go here." I wouldn't mind seeing him every day."

"You did what?"

"Listen I was just trying to start a conversation. But his rude ass tossed the damn application in my face and told me do my job and gets my boss. I would have cussed him out if he wasn't so cute."

"Kim this is the last time I'm going to tell you stop being in every man's face that comes into this establishment. We need to be professional at all times. You handing that man an employment application was disrespectful. I know you know that he doesn't need a job by his appearance. Plus, his daughter was a former student at this very daycare. Just send him in please."

"My bad boss lady," Kim responded in an annoyed tone before walking out of the room. I swear I was about to start looking for her replacement. She has one more time to do some dumb shit, I was firing her on the spot. I don't care who she's related too.

"Why do I have to hunt you down at your job?" Ira's deep voice invaded my office before he shut the door. Being in his presence made me have butterflies.

"Things have just been hectic lately."

"I'm not trying to hear that shorty. People make time for what's important to them."

"I know," I muttered feeling like a piece of shit. Ira was such a kind soul. I refused to bring him unnecessary drama and chaos in his and Troi's life. I know the way Ira is getting money is the furthest thing from legit. First thing first Ira is Angelo's right-hand man, and he's related to the Black Brothers. Sebastian being the vindictive person that he is, he'll do any and everything in his power to bring Ira down just to teach me a lesson. Troi already lost one parent I won't be the reason why she loses the other.

"I brought you lunch since you ducking me again. I thought I told you when I call you needed to answer." He said placing a Panera Bread bag on my desk.

"Thank you, you are so thoughtful." I couldn't stop the smile that was spreading across my face if I wanted too. It's been ages since I received lunch at work. It may not seem like much to some, but I truly appreciated the kind gesture.

"No problem. So wassup with you? You kind of got ghost after the movies with the girls. Troi been asking for you. She wants you to come to her dance recital this Saturday. If you can't make it, it's cool. But she would love to see you."

"Of course, I'll be there how much are the tickets?" Troi always loved to dance, and I would be honored to see her perform.

"Don't insult me. I already brought everybody's tickets. The whole family going. But after the recital, I want to take you out. No, if and or buts about it."

"I guess since you're not giving me an option," I said taking a bite out of my sandwich.

"How you know this is my favorite?

"I have my ways," He responded causing me to look at him sideways.

"Tracey told me what to get you. You just can't let a nigga have his moment."

"Nope." I laughed.

"It's cool, so you want me to pick you up from ya place before the show," He asked, and my heart dropped to the pit of o my stomach. He could never come by my house that will be the death of me if Sebastian ever found out.

"No!" I shouted causing his face to tighten up. His intense stare was as if he was looking right through me. I wonder if he could see the fear through me.

"I can just meet you there at the recital."

"You still in that situation I told you to get out."

"It's complicated," was all I could say. Nobody could understand my situation, and I didn't want to be judged. If I leave Sebastian, I lose everything. It's just not me that will be affected by my decision it's my parents also. I pay off all my parents' bills. My mother never worked; she was on disability ever since I could remember. My Father used to work for the Philadelphia Airport but has retired and is living off his pension. However, with my mom's medical bills things get tight for them, and that's where I step in. Plus, Sebastian had moved my parents out of the two-bedroom apartment we always lived into one of his many properties that he rented. I would hate for him to snatch away their stability because I pissed him off.

"Alright," Ira said and left the situation alone which I was thankful. Throughout our little unexpected lunch date, we talk about everything under the sun. He opened up to me about how he went to jail and missed the birth of Troi and how he still holds on to the guilt of not being there for Amelia in her time of need. I could only imagine how he felt getting arrested, learning that you daughter was born, but your fiancée died in the process. I know that's deep wound that will have to heal over a period of time. He has to learn to forgive himself. I told him about my upbringing. I made sure to keep Sebastian out of the conversation. The more time I spent around Ira, the more, I liked him, and I knew it would be harder to stop these growing feelings.

"Thank you for lunch." I smile standing up. He just received a phone call and told me he had to go.

"No problem. I don't like the situation that you're in. I know we haven't spoke on it. I'm just really good at reading people. When I told you that I was going to pick you up I saw nothing but fear in you. It wasn't the kind of fear that a person gets when they don't want to be caught cheating. It was more of the kind of fear of a person that is being harmed. So, I'm going to ask you is ol' boy putting his hands on you?"

I was caught off guard. Was I that transparent?

"Baby girl you wear your emotions on your face. You can let me know what's going on and I promise you it will be taken care of before the end of this night." Ira said with a straight face. I was so nervous did he just subliminally tell me that he will kill Sebastian or basically take care of Sebastian in any way he sees fit.

"What do you mean take care of it?" I asked.

"Don't worry about that. Just know he won't be a problem to you anymore." He pulled me close to him, and I just melted in his arms.

"I don't know why I have the sense to protect you, but I do. Maybe I'm trying to right some of my wrongs. It could be because you remind me of Amelia because you have a gentle soul and my daughter is so drawn to you. Or maybe it's because I know what you're deciding to go through in secrecy is not something you should be going through at all."

"If I walk away I walk away from everything." The tear was coming, and I couldn't stop them if I wanted to. I didn't want this life I had become accustomed too. I wanted to be let free of the fear of being beat because I didn't do something right or because Sebastian had a bad day at court. I wanted to be loved and protected. But how can I depend on a man who I literally only spend a couple hours with. I had to figure this out on my own. Sebastian promises to sign everything over to me when we get married. So, marrying the devil seems to be my only way out. But even that theory doesn't allow me feel safe because of who Sebastian is connected too. He is the son of the retired Police Commissioner Taylor also he himself is the state prosecutor. As sad as it was, I wasn't ready to lose everything I built. I had to find a way to get out on my own with my businesses and my parents' house with me.

"Riley..." Ira started but Kim bust through my office without knocking causing me to quickly pull away from Ira. But by the hating ass look on Kim's face, I knew she was probably about to be causing more chaos in my life.

"Umm... Riley, your fiancée, is on line one." Kim said rolling her eyes.

"You need to learn how to fucking knock before walking into her office. Baby, I'll get at you later. You definitely need to tighten up ship around here. Starting with finding someone else to fill her position."

"Excuse me."

"You heard me. Your thirsty ass is unprofessional and is a bad asset to her business." He said before turning back to me and lean down kissed me passionately. I enjoyed the moment, but I knew I was going to suffer the consequences later for my unfaithful act in front of Kim.

"Answer your phone when I call, or I will pull up to your house.

I don't give a fuck if ya nigga there or not."

"Mmmm hmm." Kim cleared her throat." Your fiancée is on the phone."

"Get at me later."

"Okay, I will," I said before he turned away from me to walk out of my office.

"Must be nice to be engaged to my cousin and still have ya fun on the side."

"It must be nice to know you only have a job because of who your cousin is. Kim don't get fucked up minding my business. Now you can excuse yourself." I dismissed her. I waited for her to leave my office before I put up the phone to speak to Sebastian.

"Yes, Sebastian I answered rudely.

"Riley baby, how are you?" he asked like just a week ago he didn't beat me up.

"I have broken ribs, Sebastian. How do you think I am?"

"I'm sorry. You just make me so mad. Riley, you kissed another man in front of me. How do you think I'm supposed to react to that. I love you so much, and sometimes I allow my anger to get the best of me because I can't lose you. I will never let you."

"Are you serious? That same day you was coming from a date with your fucking secretary!" I screamed through the phone. How dare he try to place the blame on me. Yes, me kissing Ira was not okay but this muthafucka been fucking his help for God knows how long.

"All you been doing to me is beating me since we got engaged. This is not love."

"Riley I'm sorry. Please let me make it up to you."

"How you want to make it up to me this time Sebastian flowers, jewelry, clothes, or shoes? It the same song every time with you I'm tired. I'm tired of lying to the hospital telling them stupid stories on how I received my injuries. I'm tired of living in fear I don't deserve this life. This wasn't the life you promised me."

"I know, and I'm sorry. Baby I know it's hard for you to believe me, but I promise you I will never hit you again. Can I come home tonight?"

"I think I need more time." I wanted him to stay away from me as long as I could keep him away.

"Riley I'm trying to apologize and work on our relationship. We both were wrong, and now we need to fix it. Plus, tonight is the gala that the mayor is hosting. I need you in attendance my father and mother will be there. I already I have your gown and shoes at the house already. Take half of day I already made your appointment at Reign's Day Spa so you can get your hair and nails done. I will be picking you up at six." Sebastian told me before hanging up in my ear. This is what this man calls an apology. He probably only called because of this gala we needed to attend. I hated being around his mother, and the last thing I wanted to do is play fake around snobbish people.

Chapter 14

Sebastian

"I have the tux for the Gala," Isabella said walking into her bedroom with the garment bag draped across her right arm.

"Thank you." I eyed her shapely body. Isabella had body to be a white girl. Well, a body that I paid for if I wanted to be honest. Isabella was my secretary, and she did all the nasty things that Riley would never do. That's why she will always be around.

"So, are you taking me tonight?" she asked sitting on my lap. I knew this question was going to pop up and I wasn't ready to deal with her theatrics when I told her no.

"Isabella you know when it comes to public appearances, I have to take my fiancée. So Riley is coming with me tonight. I did get you a ticket."

"So, you think I want to come to the Gala alone and watch you and your little girlfriend fake like y'all are happy. Or that you haven't been staying at my house you brought for me all week." Isabella snapped standing up and turning around to face me. I could tell she was pissed her skin was turning as red as a tomato.

"When are you going to leave her? It's been three years you been telling me you was going leave. She even knows about our affair what is keeping you with her." And there goes the waterworks.

"Isabella, Riley is my fiancée. How would it look for me to show up with my secretary? I don't need my personal laundry out to the public, and the last thing you should want is to be known as a homewrecker. Trust me our time will come; you just have to be patient."

"Okay," she muttered as I wrapped my arms around her.

"With you is where I want to be. I just need some time." I lied.

"Let me get dressed so I can pick up Riley. Isabella know your place. Riley's already going to be pissed seeing you there so don't do anything that will make her cause a scene."

It's hard keeping two women happy and satisfied. Truth was I was never leaving Riley. As messed up as I may be, I truly do love Riley. She was my first love, and that kind of love will never go away. I can't lie seeing with another man broke my heart. I never thought I'd witness Riley doing her even after all of the beatings and cheating. I never thought she would seek love from somewhere else. Riley is truly a genuine person. Most women found an interest in me because of the wealth that my family had. My mother Charlotte came from old money, and my father was the commissioner of Philadelphia's Police Department.

Riley didn't care about any of that she wanted to be with me because of me; money didn't impress her. My mother hated her, all my life my mother wanted me to marry someone who could contribute to our family's wealth. When I met Riley, she was still living on campus at Cheyney University. But during the summers and holidays, she stayed in the two-bedroom apartment with her parents. She was not the ideal mate that my mother pictured, and she let Riley know every second they are around each other.

"Okay Sebastian I'm an adult I know how to act. I don't want your little ratchet queen from the ghetto to try and beat me up." Isabella joked not knowing Riley would really throw hands. I know firsthand how Riley can fight she even gave me a black eye or busted lip before.

"I'm dead serious don't try her. She will beat your ass." I said without a smile letting her know to tread lightly. I felt bad because she actually looked petrified.

"Maybe I should just stay here."

"Yeah, I think that's best." I continued to get dressed, and around five thirty the car service was ringing Isabella's doorbell.

"You look handsome are you coming back tonight?" Isabella asked as she walked me to the door.

"No not tonight I have to make things right with Riley. We have business together, and I can't allow our relationship to go just yet." I lied. I own all of Riley's daycares, her house, her parent's house and all of their cars. This was my collateral that I always held over Riley's head. If Riley ever leaves me, she knows she and her family will be homeless. If I had to think of a word that describes Riley to the 'T' it would be utilitarianism because her actions will always be based off what's best for everybody as a whole versus what's best for her.

"Fine, I guess I'll see you at work on Monday." Isabella snapped before slamming her front door shut. I couldn't worry about her attitude right now. I had to make my way to Riley.

Pulling up to the house I am supposed to share with my fiancée a feeling of guilt overcame me. I hated that I couldn't control my anger when it came to Riley. She was the only girlfriend that I had who I put my hands on. I knew I had to change before she truly left me or worse I go too far and kill her. I would never be able to forgive myself if that happens. Getting out of the car I rang the doorbell.

"You look gorgeous." I complimented as she opened up the door and I saw her in the black gown and matching red bottoms black heels.

"Thank you." I lean in to kiss her, and she jumped from me in fear. The look on her face broke my heart. I hated that she was afraid of me. But, more sadistic as this may sound, I'd rather her live in fear of me than her leaving and me living without her love.

"Baby I'm not going to hurt you come on let's enjoy this night. I meant everything that I said on the phone. I love you Riley, and I'm going to be a better man. A man you deserve." I said, and she smiled a little before I led her to the car with our driver.

∞∞∞∞

The Mayor's Gala was being held at the Drexelbrook, and I must say it's beautiful. After being escorted to the table with my family, I knew mother was already about to be her usually stuck up self. Especially, the way she was looking at Riley. My father Sabastian Taylor Sr. was good friends with the Mayor, and we had to come to all of his events.

"Hello, son, and Riley I must say you look gorgeous this evening." My father complimented grabbing Riley's hand and spinning her in a circle causing my mother to roll her eyes.

"I think the dress is too revealing to be wearing to a formal event." My mother Abigail said in a snobbish tone.

"Oh well, your son handpicked it out for me," Riley said giving me a look telling me to get control over this situation.

"Yeah I did, I think she looks gorgeous if I do say so myself."

"Yes, son you did well for once." My father acknowledged.

The relationship between me and my father has always been a strained one. In honesty, Riley is the only thing he compliments me on. Ever since I was little, it seemed that he resented me and my mother. Anyone that was around them knew their marriage was only out of convenience. That's why my father always had affairs and didn't care about embarrassing my mother. He has been in a long-term relationship with his very own secretary Christina for the past ten years. I didn't know if my mother was oblivious to the reality sitting across the table from her; but

Christina and my father was sitting next to one another and my mother on the opposite side of the table drinking as much champagne to get her a nice buzz.

Over time growing up I stopped seeking my father acceptance and my father's approval. I wanted to be my own man, and I hated that my name connected him to me. During my whole time in law school and even at my job, some of my colleagues believe I only received my position through my father and not because I was the best candidate for the job. Being my father's child didn't have perks. Especially, when there are multiple rumors stating my father was the dirtiest cop and Commissioner the city of Philadelphia ever had in that position. Now I always have people looking at me sideways to make sure I was nothing like him. I can't tell you if the rumors are true or not but what I can tell you is I won't put nothing past him.

"Thank you for coming with me tonight," I spoke in Riley's ear as we danced in the middle of the dancefloor. The night was going on without a hitch, and we was actually laughing and enjoying one another's company.

"No problem Sebastian."

"I just want to get back to the way we were," I admitted honestly. I didn't take pleasure in beating Riley, but she just pushed me to the point of no return.

"I wasn't the one who changed. I would love to go back to how things were, but the beatings have to stop."

"They will I promise you. I love you Riley, and the last thing I want is for you to leave me." I said before the song ended. Walking back to the table I wanted to shit bricks as we came face to face with Isabella sitting next to my mother.

"You want things to change, but ya bitch is sitting next to ya mother." Riley hissed through gritted teeth.

"I don't know why she's here baby I didn't invite her." I lied. I thought Isabella was going to stay home, and even if she did come she was supposed to be at a different table than us.

"Look who I seen sitting across the room. So, you know I had to invite Isabella over here to sit with us. I thought nobody would mind." My mother said looking at Riley daring her to say something.

"I guess not since your retired husband's secretary is sitting next to him while you're sitting across the table. So, Isabella welcome to this shit show." Riley said mumbling the shit show part.

My mother was furious that her light skin was red filled with embarrassment. The thing that I didn't understand as a woman why would she flaunt Isabella in Riley's face being messy.

"What are you trying to say?" My mother asked looking between my father and Christina.

"Mrs. Taylor you a very smart woman you can figure it out. Everybody at this table has already. Now please excuse me." Riley said grabbing her purse and headed towards the exit, and of course, I followed her. I was embarrassed that she behaved in that manner and aired out my parents business in front of everyone sitting at the table. As soon as the driver pulled up we both quickly hopped in.

Slap

"How dare you speak to my mother like that!" I barked after I slapped her silly. The tears already started to form in her eyes.

"Why the fuck was your mistress there?" She screamed back starting to swing on me. I felt like I was Ike and she was Tina when they was in back of the limo going blow for blow.

"Riley chill out," I was tired and out of breath trying to restrain her.

"I hate you. Just told me you wasn't going to put your hands on me no more. You think I'm going to allow you to embarrass me like your father does ya retarded ass mother. Fuck you!"

"Tony pull up in here," I told my driver who'd been silent the whole time. I Just told him to pull up in Ricard Allen Projects. There was nothing but hoodlums and drug addicts out. I just needed a minute to calm down.

Ding

My phone altered me that I had an incoming text message.

Kim: *Hey, cousin I just wanted to let you know that your fiancée is not as innocent as you think. Maybe you should rethink marrying her. I believe she is having an affair with a man named Ira Black. He showed up today at the daycare and they spent almost two hours together with the door closed in her office. When I went to tell her, you was on the phone I saw them fixing their clothes like I just interrupted something. And when he left, he kissed her. I'm not being messy, but family look out for one another.*

Reading the text message had me tight and looking at the picture that she sent next sent me over the edge. Throwing my phone, it clocked her right in the forehead.

"What the fuck."

"You still seeing that nigga I caught you with." I barked. The looked on her face told me Kim wasn't lying. I knew she wasn't lying because of the picture she just sent me.

"Sebastian.... I'm not seeing him." She lied in my face which pissed me off even more.

"Take your clothes off," I demanded causing her to look at me like I was crazy.

"Do what the fuck I say before I beat ya ass worse than I ever did before."

Slowly but surely Riley started to unclothed looking at her vanilla skin it was coverd in black bruises. I probably would have felt regretful if she didn't piss me off and push me to the point that she does. When she was sitting in front of me in nothing but a thong, she couldn't wear a bra with the dress I picked out for her I was satisfied.

"You want to be a hoe I'll treat you as such. Get out of the car!"

"Sir." Tony started.

"Mind your business I'm the one cutting you a damn check." I snapped. Nobody had time for him to be captain save a hoe.

"Riley you heard me get the fuck out now!" I barked opening my car door. If she didn't want to get out, I would drag her dumb ass out.

Chapter 15

Ira

"Sebastian please stop! Don't do this to me!" I heard a female scream.

I'd just rolled up to collect from one of my soldiers at Richard Allen Projects. I was making sure everything was cool before I headed home to my lil mamas. I would have been left if I didn't see this Black Town car pull up. Shit looked suspicious, and I wanted to make sure nobody on my team was moving funny.

"Oh, shit you see this." One of youngbuls said pulling out his phone to record the fuckery that was taking place in front of us. A man in a tux literally dragged a female who was only in a thong and black heels out of the car. Then pushed her on ground before hopping back in the car."

"Please, Sebastian I'm sorry don't do this to me!" She begged right before he pulled off. I could hear her sobbing as she picked herself up off the ground. Whoever that nigga was had to be a cold muthafucka why would he leave shorty in the hood.

"Delete that shit," I growled to the youngbul who was recording.

"Mannnnn."

"Delete that shit. Ain't shit funny about what that nigga did. Would you be laughing if somebody did that shit to ya mom or one of your sisters. Delete that shit if I heard you posted it or anything, I'll personally fuck you up and send the video to ya momma as she pray you survive the ass whopping I'll give you." Youngbul deleted the video and showed me the proof me.

"Alright, I'm out." I fist pumped Roger he was the one in charge of the trap we had out here. Walking towards my car, I saw shorty starting to walk, and the crack heads was already on shorty ass. I usually stay out domestic violence situations, but I couldn't let shorty walk home. If I did, I knew she would have never made it, and I probably would've seen they found her body on channel six news. That was a guilt that I couldn't have on my heart. The closer I drove up on her the more familiar she became.

"Riley," I shouted out of my window causing her to turn around.

"Ira?" she said stopping dead in her tracks. I placed the car in park and hopped out. Now I was pissed. I was ready to place a bullet in her nigga's head.

"Get in the car," I said as I got out and popped my trunk and grabbed my duffle bag.

"What the fuck Riley?" I mumbled as I got back in the car and handed her the duffle bag.

"It's a clean T-shirt and ball shorts in there put them on."

"What are you doing here?" She asked getting dress. Looking her over I could see the old bruises that were healing and new ones forming on her body. I hated that she lied to me about her situation. I asked her before I left her office was her nigga putting hands on her.

"Don't worry about that. Tell me his name," was all I said, and I saw the look in her face, and I knew she wasn't about to oblige to demand.

"No, I don't want to involve you in my fucked up situation. Especially, since you're the reason for the last two ass whopping's, I got." She mumbled. She didn't say it in a blaming manner but hearing her nigga was beating on her because of me already had me ready to seal his fate.

"All I need is a name."

"No please drop it. Trust me you don't want to come for a guy like my fiancée. He will do anything to send you back to jail. I won't be the reason why you are snatched out of Troi's life. So please promise me you'll leave it alone." Riley begged me with pleading eyes. I just simply nodded because that was going to be a promise I will eventually break. I knew men like Sebastian they won't stop they love the control they have over their women.

"Are you hungry?" I asked changing the subject.

"No. I just want to go home please."

"I'm not taking you home; that shit is dead," I said with finality as I drove in the direction of my house. She let out a deep sigh and just looked out the window. I knew she was embarrassed. But there was no need. I also knew she wasn't going to give me any information on her man. That was cool too because I didn't need her to tell me anything. My last name is Black. I'll have his information down to who his parents are by tomorrow.

Seeing what happen to Riley last night had me wanting to protect her even more. To be honest, I wasn't about to let her out of my sight. Today was my baby girl's recital. So, I had Ms. Ella take her to my cousin Pharaoh's fiancée spa to get her hair done with a mani and pedi.

"You better be happy I love you Ira making me get out of bed before I had too to go shopping for ya little boo," Queen said walking inside my house with shopping bags in each hand. Early this morning I ask her to go to the mall and buy Riley some clothes, shoes, underwear and all the female personal items she would need to feel comfortable.

"Thanks, cuz."

"So, what's the deal with you and ole girl? You know she's engaged to get married."

"That shits dead," I said looking through the bags she place on the couch.

"Oh, you seem serious. You sending me to buy clothes and shit like you plan on her living up in here." Queen smiled looking at me. Everybody been waiting for me to bring somebody home and settle down. Even Queenie done found somebody, and for the longest, I really thought she was gay because she never brought a man around. But her and Kelz are going strong.

"I like shorty. Me wanting her to stay here is for her safety. I don't like her situation she got at home."

"What situation."

"Her nigga beating on her. Last night he dropped her off in the middle the of the projects ass naked."

"Do you know who her fiancée is?" Queen asked giving me a look that she knew something that I didn't.

"Naw and shorty won't tell me." I shook my head at Riley's stubbornness. I didn't understand why she would want to protect a man who caused her harm and disrespect in the worst way possible.

"Well, you know my nosey self-got the scoop on her. Especially since you woke me up early this morning asking me to go shopping for her. So, Reign told me that she engaged to Sebastian Taylor Jr. They was been together since college."

"You telling me he's the Commissioner's son?"

"Yup, so you know things can get messy dealing with her. Commissioner Taylor Sr. may not be the commissioner anymore, but his son is the state prosecutor. His son is nothing like him; he's actually on the straight and narrow. There's nothing dirty about him. As a matter of fact, he's known for going for the jugular. Every person he prosecutes they always get the maximum sentence."

"Thanks for the information," I said not caring who Sebastian was and what his job description entailed. I was going to handle him off GP. He was a bitch made nigga pulling stunts like he did yesterday.

"So, what are you going to do with that information." Queen inquired with raised eyebrows.

"I'm going to handle her situation that she calls a relationship."

"Ira, I know you like her probably even care for her even though you won't admit it. But you need to approach this situation with open eyes and with caution. As of now, she is in a toxic domestic violence relationship. You and I both know this wasn't the first time he beat or degraded her, yet she's still engaged to be married to this man. He's has control over her that only she can take back. It will be up to her to walk away from him."

"Riley can't go back to him after what he did last night," I said more to myself. If she did, I would honestly look at her differently. How many times does a man have to disrespect and put hands on you to realize it's time to walk away.

"Walking away isn't that easy. It, not all black and white how many people think. That's why you have to handle this differently. There's no need to put a target on yours or the family's back only for her to run back into his arms. You have too much to lose. It's not just you, you have Troi to think about." Queen said

"I know."

"Let me get out of here. I have to pick Charlie up from the spa. Then Kelz is taking us out for lunch before the recital." She said giving me a hug before she walked out the front door.

"Thanks again. I'll see y'all in a couple hours," I called to her back as she walked to her car.

Grabbing the shopping bags, I walked upstairs to my bedroom. I allowed Riley to sleep in there last night because my bed was way more comfortable than the guest bedroom. Riley ws sleeping so peaceful it seemed like this was the first time in a long time she had a good night's sleep.

"Riley," I called her name as I placed the bags on the bed.

"Riley," this time I shook her. Riley jump up in a sitting up position with the most terrified look. I could tell she was scared. It wasn't until she recognized me that she started to calm down. Her reaction only made me want to get at Sebastian even more. It's crazy that he had her this scared this was no way to live.

"Why would you scare me like that?" she hissed. I knew her anger was more out of embarrassment.

"I didn't mean to scare you. I bought you some clothes, shoes, and personal items you will need while you stay here."

"Ira you didn't have to do all of that, I'm not a charity case. Plus, I will be out of your hair soon. I didn't plan on staying." She said getting up to look in the bags and grabbed the toothbrush. And made her way into my personal bathroom and started brushing her teeth and washing her face. Hearing those word slip past her lips had me heated.

"So, you just going to go back to that nigga that beat your ass on the daily basis's. You okay with going back to the muthafucka who dropped you off in the middle of the hood ass naked. And was okay with you walking home not caring if you get raped or murdered in the process. Trust you was going to get rape if I wasn't there to help you. The crackhead and homeless niggas were already following you." I barked causing her to jump back away from me.

"Don't judge me!" she screamed.

"Ira you don't know my life or struggle. I can't just walk away. I will lose everything."

You keep saying you will lose everything. What are you losing?" I asked.

"I'll lose everything I worked hard for. I will lose all of my daycares all five of them. Not only will I lose my businesses that I built from the ground up. I will lose my house, car and so will my parents because all of our houses and cars are in Sebastian's name. I know it may sound stupid to you. But I was in love with this man engaged to be married. I never thought he would turn into this monster. He was helping me and my family. I never thought he would turn his help into something to keep me from leaving. Even if I do leave it will be too hard for all of us to start over," she admitted.

"Let me help you." I offered. After hearing her reason, I realize shorty had the weight of the world on her shoulders. Any decision that she made will not only affect her. But I'm willing to help."

"You help me? Ira, you barely know me. Plus, I learned my lesson about allowing a man to help me or my family. That's why I'm in this predicament I'm in now."

I could tell that Riley was untrusting and she had every right to be. After her experience with Sebastian, she'll probably never trusts another man again. But I'm not him. If she stays in this relationship, it will only leads to her death.

"Riley don't compare me to that nigga. Whatever I do for you will be done with no strings attached. I just want you safe. If me helping you and your parents is what makes you safe consider it done." I said with confidence.

"Helping me will only bring unnecessary drama to your life."

Riley's constant needs to protect everybody is what is attracting me to her even more. She is such a selfless person. However, this great quality can be her major fault. To be honest her parents were adults, and she shouldn't be carrying the burden of caring for them. Especially, when they are perfectly able to care for themselves. Then again, I understand her reason. If my mother was still alive, there was nothing anyone can say to stop me from helping her.

"Riley I'm a man; and my name is Ira Black. I can handle a weak ass nigga like Sebastian. Stop worrying about me. You need to start figuring out how you going to gain back control of your life. Just tell me you're ready to take the step of leaving your abuser and I promise to be by your side every step of the way."

Riley look me dead in my eyes. I guess she was trying to read me to see if I was bullshitting her. But I'm not, and sooner than later she will find out I'm a man of my word.

"I'm ready." She said with a little hope in her voice.

That all I needed to hear. Now I had to talk with my Aunt Maria and Uncle Royal on how I should approach this situation. I know killing Sebastian was not going to be their answer because his father knew too much of the family. His knowledge can be my family's downfall.

Chapter 16

Mason

"**M**ason, you have any reason why your brother wanted to see you today?" Desi inquired.

We were currently on the road to Graterford Prison. Desi was visiting her cousin Pookie, and I was visiting my brother Mike. This is where my brother Mike called home for the past nine years. He only had one more year to go and he would be a free man. My brother was the only family I had beside Desi. I considered Austin and Peanut family too, but those niggas been ghost lately. The only person I had in my corner now was my wife. It's true when they say the realest person on you team is ya girl.

"I don't know he made it seem urgent as hell that I came."

When my brother called me yesterday, he made it seem like I had to drop everything to make sure I was at the prison for visitation hours. Whatever he had to tell me he acted as though he couldn't tell me over the phone. So, I knew it was serious.

"I guess we'll find out when we get there. But what I really wanted to talk to you about is when are we hitting our next lick and who's it's going to be? We need to move ASAP."

"Desi, I know," I muttered in frustration. Lately, Desi has been on my ass nagging me about making money. Not only was she constantly in my ear annoying the fuck out of me. My team that I was trying to build had fallen apart.

"Don't get an attitude with me. You're not the one selling pussy to make sure our head stay above water." Desi snapped.

There was nothing I could say because everything Desi said was true. I basically been pimping my own wife out just to pay our rent and car notes. Things had gone from bad to worse since the night at the club. Most of our licks came from Desi's customers that she would run game on at the strip club. But ever since King fired her from KING's. Money been tight and this new strip club she been working at she was barely bring home three hundred dollars a night.

"What did you have in mind? Do you have a person that's going to have a nice come up."

"I sure do." She said with a sneaky smile.

"Who?"

"I have a couple people in mind. I have two johns that have been seeing me on the regular. They have a little change that we can snatch. But our main target needs to be Peanut." I was a grimy nigga but damn going after one of my niggas I grew up with was foul as fuck. She must have noticed my face because she started to explain.

"Don't look at me like that Mason. Peanut is out for himself and only himself." Desi said.

"What do you know that I don't?" I asked. I haven't spoken to Peanut since the night our so-called meeting was supposed to go down with Majesty. I figured he was still in his feelings. It was nothing for Peanut to hold grudges.

"Well, I saw him recently and he was looking like money. I asked him wassup, and he told me he was now working with his cousins Aquil and Law selling guns. When I asked why he didn't put you and Austin on, he told me he wasn't fucking with you." Desi answer and the wheels were already turning in my head. Peanut is foul for making moves and not putting us on. There was plenty of time he was eating because of me. But the thing that stood out to me the most was where the fuck she see Peanut.

"So, are you going to tell me where you see Peanut and why were you talking to him?" For Desi to get the information from Peanut, he must feel like he could have trusted her. Peanut always been secretive so, me not knowing about his new business venture was no shock to me. But him speaking his personal business with Desi had me side eyeing her.

"What are you trying to insinuate Mason? I saw him coming out of the barbershop. You already know I'm cool with all of your friends."

"Yeah okay."

We continued the rest of the ride to the prison with the radio playing. As of right now, I couldn't worry about Desi and Peanut. At the end of the day she wanted me to rob him. Robbing Peanut may be the move I need to make. I know his cousins Law and Aquil are making big money selling guns the legit and illegal way. They even own a gun range in South Philly. I hated coming up to prison.I hated the whole process of checking in. But for Mike, I will do anything. My brother always had my back. So, for him, I'll make this dreadful trip.

Once we were process in me, and Desi took seats at different tables as we waited for the inmates to come to the visitor's room. Ten minutes of sitting I saw my brother walking through the doors. Usually, he would be happy to see a nigga. But the stone look he had on his face told me otherwise.

"Wassup Mike," I said as he pulled me in for her hug.

"Nigga you tell me I see you still fucking with that snake ass bitch Desi." He said before we sat down.

"Man, she's my wife and the mother of my child." I stated shaking my head. Mike never hid his disdain for Desi.

"Yeah, I don't know why you did that bullshit either. But how's my nephew? Why don't you bring him to visit me?" he asked, and I felt like shit. How could I look my brother in the face to tell him

I'm a fucked up individual and I wasn't man enough to raise him and that Desi mother has custody of him. Shit, I couldn't even tell him anything about my son.

"I'll bring him next time. The way you sounded on the phone you sound like we needed to discuss serious business."

"We do, you need to chill the fuck out. You're out there claiming GMM. You know damn well Angelo want ya head. Mason, I can't protect you from in here. Blue came to me talking about Angelo is ready to put a fucking bullet in your head. Blue was able to talk him off the ledge, but just know I'm all out a favors. You need to chill and watch your back. Just because Angelo agreed not to kill you don't mean he letting you slide."

I just nodded because that was the last thing, I needed to be doing is looking over my fucking shoulder for Angelo's deranged ass. I heard about all the horror stories about what happened in his cabin on the outskirt of Philly.

"You only got on more year left."

"Yeah, I'm ready to get the fuck up out of here." He said smiling for the first time.

"I can't wait until you get home. Then we'll be seeing some real money.

"Naw... You already know when I come home, I'm not going to be a part of GMM. From what I hear up in here is that they basically run Philly. The Black brothers only do business with them, and you already know Angelo not fucking with me. It's nothing personal I'm just bad for their business because of my relation to you."

"That's fucked up." I hissed. Angelo been getting on my nerves for the last couple years thinking he's the street God.

"You started GMM."

"Mason, I didn't start shit that was all Sean and Blue. They looked out because of our living situation with mom dukes. They put me in a position to get money, but I blew it over a dice game. I'm in my late thirties I'm not about to get out of jail just to start gang banging. I picked up a trade in construction. I'm going to try to put that shit to use. Start my own business because you know nobody about to hiring a felon."

"I hear you. That's wassup." Man, some people would be happy that when their loved ones was coming home from jail they wanted to stay on the straight and narrow. But not me I was depending on Mike to help me make some moves to get put on. I didn't see myself working a 9-5 that's the main reason why I was out here being a jack boy.

"Who's the nigga that's sitting with ya wife," Mike asked looking in Desi direction; she saw him and smiled. He only hit her with the head nod.

"What fuck happen to her teeth."

"Ol' boy is her cousin Pookie that the nigga who put me on."

"You mean the nigga who put you on to the DEA." Mike hissed. He hated the whole situation because it ended up with me going back to jail, but Tracey took the bid for me. He voiced his opinion plenty of time how he hated the way I dogged Tracey.

"Till this day that situation sounded like a whole set up. I'm going to figure that shit out though. He already have a reputation of being a snitch." I hope Pookie wasn't on no bullshit I trusted him. I never thought he would be on some snake shit like getting me caught up because I had his own cousin making the drops and pickups.

"But what happened to shorty's teeth."

"Angelo is what happens. Desi called herself talking crazy to Tracey after Tracey beat her up."

"I didn't know shorty was released. Why would she even talk to the girl after the nut shit y'all put her through." Mike said shaking his head. I said the same thing I hated that Desi even made her presence known. Seeing Tracey at the club that night made me feel like shit. All I wanted was the opportunity to apologize. For the last past five years, I put Tracey in the back of my mind so my guilt wouldn't get to me.

"Man, I don't know." I groaned.

"All I know is Tracey beat her ass after Desi went over there taking shit. Then she started talking about pressing charges. So, Angelo rammed his gun in her mouth knocking out her front teeth." I explained.

"What you do?" he asked.

"What could I do GMM was in there deep. I wanted to live to see another day. I wasn't going to give him a reason to blast my ass. Plus, Desi deserved that shit."

"Hmmm. You're right, but you still went out like a punk. But that's neither here nor there. I'm going to find out what really went down on the drop with her cousin and the DEA. That shit never sat right with me. And to be honest, everybody needs to learn the truth. Plus, I think you need to apologize to Tracey. Her life change riding for you and you did her dirty. She may not want to hear it, but you need to say it." Mike said before changing the subject. For the rest of the visit we talked about him coming home and the plan, we were going to make when he touched down.

$$\infty\infty\infty$$

I just walked into Cutz it's the barbershop everybody goes to in Philly. Its own by Nasir he had a chain of barbershops throughout Philly, but I only allowed him to cut my hair. And he only cut in the shop in West Philly. Taking a seat, I see Peanut and Austin waiting for their barber to cut their hair.

"Long time no see or hear niggas."

"Wassup" Austin spoke, and Peanut just nodded his head.

"Yo I'm ready for you," Nasir called out to me.

"So why everybody been ghost. I hit both of you up and got no answer." I asked. Ever since my visit with my brother I've been walking on eggshells knowing Angelo was in the shadows somewhere lurking waiting to make his move. What got me looking at everybody sideways is the fact that my right and left-hand man dropped off the face of the earth. This was the time we needed to start thinking of a master plan.

"I just been working," Austin said, and I cocked my head to the side. Where the hell this nigga been working? Just a month or so ago he was trying get money just like me. Asking me to put him on every lick that I get.

"I just got hired at this accounting firm downtown. I finally landed a job in my degree. Shit, a nigga was starting to think I went to school for nothing." Austin answered. If I wasn't a hating ass nigga I probably would be happy for him. But all I could see is him not being able to help me with the lick I was trying to set up because he gone legit.

"Austin, I don't know why you even explaining ya self to this nigga. You're a grown ass man." Peanut hissed looking at Austin like he was crazy.

"You still in ya feeling about the night in club? That's why you decided to start working with your cousin and couldn't put family on." I asked chuckling Peanut could always hold a grudge.

"Naw I ain't mad about shit. You the one with a target on ya back. Especially, with the truth, I know about what really went down with Tracey the night she got locked up. You better hope I act like my name is Bennet and I'm not in it because death would definitely be knocking on your door."

"What the fuck you say." I hope I didn't hear him correctly.

"Tell ya, bitch, to keep my name out her mouth. Desi grill still fucked up yet she running her dick suckers like she ain't got missing teeth. How you let that nigga Angelo knock ya wife teeth out without any consequences. What makes matter first she out her asking me to get her shit fix like she swallowing my kids." Peanut snapped causing me to stand up out of Nasir chair.

"We have kids up in here," Nasir said looking all of us up and down daring up to start a fight in his barbershop. Looking around there were kids sitting waiting to get their haircuts.

"Yo I'm out. Tell Speedy I'll be back later." Peanut said referring to his barber. He shook Austin's hand and made his way out of the barbershop. I was beyond pissed that whatever plan Desi had in mind for Peanut I was all the way in. And since Desi on some snake shit herself, I'm just going to keep the money for myself. And continue to pimp her dumb ass out until she become worthless.

Chapter 17

Brooklyn

"So what y'all hoes been up too," I said to Tracey and Riley we all were at *Fridays* o for drinks and food. I been so busy that I haven't gotten a chance to kick it with my homegirls.

"Girl so much has been going on. I don't even know where to start." Riley stressed shaking her head.

"Well let's start off with you living with Ira," Tracey said spilling the tea giving Riley the side eyes.

"Damn where the hell I been you left Sebastian undercover psycho ass and got with a real nigga. Okay Riley." I joked, and Tracey bust out laughing. However, Riley didn't even crack a smile; instead her eyes filled up with tears.

"What's wrong we were just joking?" Tracey asked concerned. Riley's never been a sensitive person. We throw jabs at Sebastian all the time it never came to the point that the little jabs we throw at Sebastian would make her cry.

"Riley I'm sorry. I didn't mean to upset you. I may not like who you are in a relationship with, but if he's the one who make you happy, I'm happy." I apologize.

"No, y'all just don't know I've been staying with Ira because Sebastian was beating my ass."

"What!" Tracey said pulling out her phone.

"Tracey, what are you doing?" Riley panicked. Seeing her in

this state made me want to shoot Sebastian's ass myself. I would have never thought Riley would be in an abusive relationship.

"I'm calling Angelo they going to take care of him. I knew that nigga was putting hands on you. "

"No, I had to beg Ira not to take care of him. Let me handle Sebastian. The last thing you want to do is put Angelo in the position to have a target on his back."

"Okay, so when did this start?" I asked. Riley never showed any signs that she was getting abused. I felt like a bad friend for not noticing something was going on so tragic in her personal life.

"The abuse started after he asked me for my hand in marriage. Its gotten worse since he opened up the daycares for me. He won't let me go. This last time he kicked me out in the middle of some project's ass naked. That's when I saw Ira. He took me to his home, and I've been there ever since."

"Riley, Sebastian needs to get dealt with. What you think is going to happen when you don't go home?" I asked.

"I don't know I just need time to think. As of now, he has no way to get in contact with me. and I haven't been going into none of the daycares. I spoke with Sheila, and she's been overseeing everything for me at all of the sites." She explained.

"It's crazy because he can cheat on me, disrespect me, and the one time he finds out about Ira he beat my ass." Riley shook her head in disbelief.

"You know men can never take what they dish out. But how the hell he find out about Ira?" Tracey asked putting her phone away.

"Girl, the first time he saw me walking out the movies with him and his daughter. Then this time his hoe ass cousin Kim probably told him Ira stop by the daycare to bring me lunch. I tried to stay away from Ira, but that nigga came searching for me." Riley chuckled.

"When we done we have to pay Kim a little visit. Shorty need to catch these hands for snitching you out to Sebastian." I said already on go. I hate people minding other people's business.

"Daycare closes at six," Riley said letting me know it's a go.

"But anyway, in other news why the hell is Cream hounding us about you?"

"Yassss what did you do to that man?" Tracey said as we all bust out laughing.

Cream been a thought I been trying to push into the back of my mind. Cream was a man that I had to stay away from. The way he laid the pipe had me scared straight. Cream wasn't a man I needed to fall in love with. Everything about him was screaming run bitch! I know for a fact this nigga would probably ruin my life and leave me heart broken. That's why I dipped out his little condo before he could wake up. I know he probably have some crazy bitches that would do anything to keep him. If he didn't I damn sure didn't want to turn into that crazy bitch.

"Let just say he came down to KING's and saw me strip. I ended up at his house with my legs behind my head. Then I dipped out before he could wake up." I answer honestly.

"So ya hot ass threw the pussy on then went MIA on hi sass." Tracey shook her head.

"You must have gold between your legs I never seen Cream so damn press over any female."

"That man ain't worried about me," I said trying to hide my smile.

"The hell he ain't. I swear he asked me about you five different times in. five different ways during Troi dance recital." Riley laughed.

"Whatever I don't need a man like that in my life. But wassup with you and Angelo did you throw that ass in a circle for him."

"You know I had to make it official with his crazy ass. I'm not even going to tell y'all how this nigga basically kidnapped my dad at gunpoint and brought him to my house to make him apologize,"

"No, he did not." Riley gasped in disbelief. I wouldn't put anything pass Angelo after witnessing him knock Desi teeth out without hesitation.

"Girl yes my mom called me crying asking me was I safe with Angelo. All I could do was apologize for his behavior." Tracey said shaking her head. I could see now she had her hands full with Angelo. But I'm happy she finally got somebody who's going to ride for her. With everything she been through she deserve to be happy.

"It's good to hear you, and your mom are back on good terms," I mentioned. Tracey and Ms. Tanya always had a great relationship. To be honest, I personally envy their relationship due to the fact that I never experience that with my own mother.

"Yeah only if my dad comes around. Everything would be back to normal. Just like it was before Mason and the nonsense he brought to my life. But after the little stunt Angelo pulled, he probably needs more time to get over that."

"He will," Riley assured Tracey as we finish our food and drinks.

"It'sfive thirty," Riley announced she was pumped and couldn't wait to put her hands-on Kim.

"Y'all ready to make our way to the daycare?

"Yup," me and Tracey said in unison as we all downed the rest of our drinks

I hated to see my friend fight and usually wouldn't encourage it, but Kim deserve this ass whopping Riley was about to hand to her. I hated messy bitches. Kim's little snitching ass caused my best friend humiliation and a beat down by a man who supposedly wanted to spend the rest of his life with her. After paying the bill, we hopped in our cars and drove to our destination. When we pulled up, we saw Kim locking up the daycare's front doors.

"Kim!" Riley barked as Kim was pulling down the gate in front of the windows.

"Oh my god! Riley, you scared me. Where have you been? Sebastian has been going crazy looking for you." Kim fake concerned but we all knew the truth. Sebastian was probably scared shitless that something bad happened to Riley after he abandoned her ass naked in the hood.

"Didn't I tell you to mind your business," Riley asked calmly.

"Excuse me? Riley, I have no clue about what you're talking about."

"Hoe you know what she talking about." I snapped. I see this bitch want to play dumb now she being confronted.

"Sweetheart I don't all I know what you or ya little friends are talking about. But my cousin is worried sick. So, I'm going to call Sebastian and let him know you are safe and to come to the daycare." Kim pulled out her phone only for Tracey to smack the phone out of her hand and it smashed on the ground.

"What the fuck!"

"Bitch nobody told you to contact his bitch ass." Tracey hissed.

"Riley what you and ya friends call yourselves doing. I ain't scared of y'all." Kim screamed.

Riley didn't have anything else to say as she swung, and her fist connected to Kim's jaw. Kim stood in shock as Riley landed another punch to her right eyes. It was like reality hit Kim as she tried to defend herself from Riley's vicious punches that were raining all over her.

"Fuck her up Riley!" I encouraged watching Riley go ham. It seemed like Riley was taking out all of her pent-up aggression out on Kim. After another five minutes of Kim begging Riley to stop. Tracey and I finally pulled Riley off her.

"Damn Riley you beat the damn breaks off this girl," Tracey said looking at a sobbing Kim. Kim nose and lip was busted, and shorty had a lump above her right eyes, and the left eyes was swollen shut.

"Fuck her" Riley hissed catching her breath snatching the day-care keys off the ground because Kim dropped them.

"Strip."

"Oh shit," Tracey muttered. Kim looked up out of her one good eye and shook her head no. If you weren't close to Riley, you would think she was sweetest person alive. But being best friends with her for ten plus years I knew she had a serious mean streak running through her body.

"Bitch you running a mouth to your cousin caused him to beat my ass, make me strip naked and he dropped me off in the middle of the projects. The way I look at it is you're the reason for him humiliating me all because Ira wasn't checking for ya chicken finger shape body having ass. So, I think it's only fair that I give you the same experience."

I was down for whatever. Riley's mean streak didn't show until you fucked with her and in her eyes; Kim did the unthinkable. Looking at Tracey, we was on the same page. We both stalked over to Kim and started stripping her of her clothes until she was ass naked. Riley popped her trunk, and we dragged Kim over to her car and pushed her into the trunk.

"Bitch what we about to do I ain't trying to go back to jail again," Tracey muttered.

"We're not," I assured her.

"Angelo is gong to kick my ass fucking with y'all." Tracey let out a nervous chuckle. All I could do was shake my head because as soon as Angelo hear about our festivities, he probably going to kick all of our asses.

Riley hopped in the driving seat in her car, so we did the same. Me and Tracey both pulled our cars out of Riley's employee parking lot. But Riley decided she was apart of the fast and the furious and started doing crazy donuts in her car around the parking lot. I knew Kim was getting even more beat up in Riley's trunk after two minutes Riley finally pulled out of the lot and pull beside us and told us to follow her. We followed for about a half an hour before we Pulled into the Richard Allen Projects. It was a Friday night, and the projects was all the way live. Getting out our car. Riley popped open her trunk and well all pulled Kim out on the ground. Kim was a bloody mess begging for us not to leave her here.

"I begged your cousin not to leave me here too," Riley hissed before kicking Kim in the face. L her sobbing on the ground. Hopping back in our cars we pulled off in separate directions like nothing ever happen.

"Wassup Honey?" King asked as I walked into the strip club.

"Nothing about to get back on my money chase," I answered, and he nodded.

"What them grades looking like?" He asked. That's why I love working here, King truly cared about his workers. Most people that run a business-like KING's would see the females that work at the establishment as disposable. But not King he had all of the girl's best interest at heart. I remember when I was fucking up in school; that nigga made me stop working until I brought him some passing grades. Like what boss does that. A couple years ago some bitch name Kari owed this pimp Snake a lot of money. You probably read about her grimy ass In Allie Marie's book *Foolish Of Me*. She basically recruited some of the girls to do some work for him. Kari made it seem like he was some big shot with mad money. He was supposed to be setting the girls up with little gigs. But the Snake character had these girls straight prostituting. As soon as word got around to King, he handled it, and they never had to worry about Snake again.

"You already know I made Dean's List. Senior year going to be a breeze for me." I said smiling.

"That's what I like to hear."

"Sorry, I'm late King." I familiar voice said in our direction.

"Brooklyn?" Turning around to face the person who just called my name and it was no other than a beautiful blast from my past.

"Amira? Oh my god!" I couldn't even stop the smile from spreading across my face.

Me and Amira have history together. Amira was the first girl I gave my heart too. What we had was indescribable. Amira allowed me to be me without any judgment for my choices. She taught me how to accept my sexuality. Before her, I was in the closet ashamed of the feelings and attraction I had towards other women. Now I love the person I've become and will never hide my true self again. Me and Amira story ended when she decided to go to college in New York. She wanted to stay together, and we have a long-distance relationship. But the way both of our sexual appetites were there was no need to fake like that was a great idea. I love sex, and so did Amira we both was bi, and there was times we had threesome with a man to scratch our itch of craving for some real dick. Threesomes were something we did together so it wouldn't feel like we were cheating. But with Amira miles away I knew we would cheat on one another; with another man or worse another woman.

duced us with a smirk.

"Amira he be slanging hella dick." All I could do was shake my head at her bluntness.

"Hey Cream," Amira spoke, and I just hit her with the head nod.

"So, are you trying to come chill with me after I get off tonight?" Brooklyn asked rubbing her hand up and down my arm.

"Yeah."

"Cool, I'll text you my address to meet me at my house." She said before walking away towards VIP. I took that as my que to bounce. I decided to head on to my condo in the city to shower and smoke some weed as I waited for Brooklyn to hit me up to come over.

Walking up to my front door something was off. The lights were on in the condo, and I could hear music playing. Pulling out my gun I unlocked my door and entered my condo ready to blast the first person I see.

"It looks to be the man of the hour has arrived." Some Uncle Phil looking muthafucka said in a sarcastic tone. All I seen was red because I didn't know who this fuck nigga was yet he in my house sitting on my couch watching my damn Netflix. Walking up to him I pistol whipped him several times.

"Oh My God!" I heard another voice come from the kitchen of my apartment.

"Cream what the hell you are doing to my father!" Jodi screamed as she and an older version of herself rush over to the Uncle Phil looking nigga that was leaking on my couch.

"Bitch why the fuck is your crazy ass is in my house like you live here," I said cocking my gun and placing it to Jodi;s head. I swear I wanted to kill this bitch. But killing her will result in s triple homicide that I don't feel like cleaning the fuck up.

"Please Cream why are you treating me like this." She cried out.

"All I wanted to do was for you to meet my parents."

"Why the fuck would I want to meet these muthafuckas you almost got ya father's wig pushed back." I hissed tapping her head with the gun with every word I spoke.

"How the fuck you get in here?"

"Baby you gave me a key remember," Jodi said in between sobs.

"I ain't give you shit." I know I didn't give her delusional ass a damn key. The only thing that came to mind is that she made a copy of my key. Thinking back, I couldn't find my key to my condo last week. I had to get the spare from my mother. It just so happen when Jodi was cleaning the condo up last week it magically appeared from under the couch.

"Please put the gun down. Jodi what do you have me, and your father mixed up in." Her mother begged me and chastised her at the same time.

"What the fuck is that smell?" I muttered as I started smelling something burning and smoke.

"I was making dinner."

"Oh, my God! Jodi the pork chops." Her mom screamed and ran into the kitchen. I guess to turn off the stove and control whatever fire that this bitch probably started in my shit.

"Bitch I know ya dumb ass not cooking swine in my pots." I never ate pork a day in my life. So just hearing that she thought it was okay to cook this shit in my kitchen had me heated.

"Jodi this is the man you want us to meet?" Her father started but was cut off by his wife.

"I turned everything off. The pork chops are burned, I mean not edible. So, I don't know what we are going to eat meat wise."

"If y'all don't get y'all ass out of my crib and take your crazy ass daughter with you."

"You are so rude how can you talk to her like that?" Her mom had the nerve to ask me.

"She is your girlfriend the girl you claim to love."

I was completely thrown off by her comment. I couldn't believe Jodi was out here creating a false reality. Her parents looked at me like I lost my mind.

"I thought I told you to never settle for less. First, he attacks me, pulls a gun out on you scaring your mother half to death. On top of that this ungrateful bastard doesn't even care for the time you've taken out your day to prepare this meal."

"Come on honey we need to get you to the hospital." Jodi's mother said helping her husband to stand.

"Don't be surprised if we press charges for assault. Jodi, I can't believe you wasted our time."

"Press charges on me?" All I could do was laugh in her mom's face.

"Naw how about I call the cop on you ya husband and Jodi for trespassing I don't even know how this bitch got in my condo. I not her boyfriend the only thing I use ya daughter for was to suck my dick. Fuck with me if you want; I bet all y'all muthafuckas come up missing." I walked to the door opening it so they could make their exit.

Jodi's parents shared a look then look at Jodi who was walking towards the door with her head down.

"Jodi please don't tell me you're on this bullshit again" Her father snapped. I guess this wasn't the first time Jodi decided to go crazy over some dick.

"Mom and dad, it's not what you think. It's not like last time."

Last time I thought. So, these muthafuckas knew Jodi was a few screws missing from completion.

I truly love him.. he's just upset because I didn't let him know my plans." Jodi cried. I was over the whole scene.

"Listen we are sorry. We didn't know that we were breaking an entering. You will never see us or her again." He mother said beyond embarrassed by her daughter's actions. I didn't even acknowledge her apology just open my door wider silently letting them know to get the fuck out. I already knew I was about have to break my lease. I could easily get the locks changed, but from the look on Jodi parents face it seemed like she'd be flirting with a thin line between love and hate.

I grabbed a black trash bag from underneath the counter and just started tossing all of my pots out. Besides her cooking pork the pots she burnt up from her leaving them on the stove. I'm surprised this bitch didn't start a grease fire. After cleaning my kitchen and taking a shower, Brooklyn sent me a text. The way I was feeling I wanted to tell her I'll get up with her another time, but I didn't want to take a chance of shorty going ghost on me again. As soon as I pulled in her driveway she hit me with another text.

Brooklyn: *The key is under the mat let yourself in. I'm in the bedroom. I don't feel like coming downstairs.*

All I could do was shake my head at her lazy ass. Doing as she told me I let myself in. Walking into her house she had it decorated all nice. It was just girly as fuck. Shorty whole living scheme was black, sliver and pink. Making my way upstairs her door was cracked.

"This how you show your hospitality," I asked walking into the bedroom. The sight in front of me had me lost for words. Both Brooklyn and Amira was sitting on bed ass naked waiting for me. Amira couldn't keep her lips or hands-off Brooklyn as she kissed her along the side of her and grab a handful of her breast.

"Are you going to join us or watch us?" Brooklyn asked as she spread her legs wide open for Amira to slide in between and start eating her pussy. To be honest I wanted to do both. By the sex faces Brooklyn was making I knew Amira was handling business. My dick was on brick as I undressed. This was exactly what I needed to get my mind of the fuckery that happen a couple hours prior.

"Come here daddy I know little daddy missed me." Brooklyn moaned before Amira made her cum.

"Damn I missed the way you taste." Amira smirked licking Brooklyn juices off her lips.

"Fuck," I muttered watching them like I was on the set of a porno. I wasted no time getting on the bed with the both of them. I laid flat on my back and Brooklyn straddle my waist with my dick at her moist opening. I tapped Amira on her ass and directed her to straddle my face.

"Shit... Cream." Brooklyn let out a passionate whimper as she slide down slowly on my dick. She took her time adjusting to my length or width.

"Oh, my God...." Amira moaned as soon as my tongue connected to her clit.

Brooklyn is going to fuck around and make me wife her ass up. Shorty was a freak but not a hoe, and that was right up my alley. There was no reason to cheat when she was down with sleeping with other bitches. Yeah, our little situation may work out.

Chapter 19

Peanut

"**W**assup King," Law said as we walked up to one of the Black brothers. King was my cousin's Law and Aquil's gun supplier.

"Wassup thanks for coming out," King said, and he dapped Law and Aquil up.

We were currently at Blacks Annual End of the School Year block party. They throw this every year for the kids and parents of the neighborhood. I respect how the Black's always give back to their community. Every year you'll see every hustler out there helping in some kind of way. I always went as a kid when their father Royal started it twenty years ago.

"Who this?" he asked nodding in my direction.

"This our little cousin Peanut. He just joined us he learning the ropes. You know we trying to expand and we don't trust easily." Law said.

"That's wassup keeping it in the family. Just know blood don't always make you family or loyal." He said before dapping me up. I wasn't sure if he was just spitting knowledge or there was an underline meaning to his statement.

"You use to run around with that nigga Mason." He questioned.

"Back in the day we use to be cool, but I don't like the way he move so I don't fuck with him," I answered honestly. Why lie it was obvious he knew some of my background.

"Good to hear that." He said before telling us to follow him. He had us working the concession stand. Everybody was enjoying their selves. As it started getting late, the parents took their children, and the block party turned into a big kick back. Anybody that was somebody in the game had showed up; it was even some people from out of state that came through. So you already know the birds was out trying to catch a baller. It felt good being in the midst of real niggas. Every single person was making money and not on some crab syndrome bullshit. Thinking back I don't even know why I was hanging heavy with Mason. He never wanted to work to build something. To be honest, I looked at that nigga different when he played Desi for Tracey. But seeing him let Tracey take that bid for him was when I truly lost all respect for him.

"Peanut?" I heard my name being called. Looking up it was nobody but Desi.

"Who the fuck is that?" Aquil asked. I swear this nigga was always angry. He's known throughout the hood as the North Philly Bully. It wasn't a time when you didn't see this nigga snapping the fuck out or beating somebody ass. My cousin was a straight beast, and I don't know nobody who wanted to be on his bad side including me.

"Some jawn from around the way I know," I answered hoping Desi could take the hint and don't bring her ass over here. The last thing I wanted was King or somebody to recognize her. The word on the street is Tracey is Reign's little cousin, and Reign is Pharaoh's girl. Knowing Desi's connection to Mason I didn't want no assumptions being made about me.

"Get that bitch from around me her eyes shifty as muthafucka. I fuck around and shoot her just because..." Aquil snapped.

"Peanut don't let that girl come over here. All it take for her to look at him sideways before his trigger-happy ass shoots." Law may seem like he was joking, but anybody who knew Aquil knew Law was giving full warning.

"Desi wassup?" I said walking up to her and pulling her off to side away from everybody. I decided the best place for us to be was in my car unseen from everybody.

"Wassup with you I see you doing big things chilling with big people," Desi said sarcastically once we got in the car.

"Why the fuck you call me over here? I already told you whatever we had was done. Especially, since I know how you move." I hissed.

"I left Mason." She said putting her head down.

You know if I heard those words a couple months ago a nigga probably would have been ecstatic. See I was the first one to spot Desi way before Mason. When I pointed her out to Austin and Mason, of course, Mason made his way over there to speak to her and they been together ever since. I thought I would finally have my chance with her when Mason dropped her like a bad habit to talk to Tracey. The first time we slept together, it was on some drunk shit. She came over my crib, and we was going shot for shot. Only for her to end up face down ass up on my bed. After the first time me and Desi had sex we kept it going. Of course, my feelings started to grow. In my eyes Desi should have been my girl from get. I thought things were good until she popped up pregnant. I just knew her son was mines until she confirmed that she'd still been sleeping with Mason. I was on some straight sucker shit. Looking back on our situation I was willing to be her side nigga just to have a piece of her.

"So..."

"Peanut I know you have your doubts about me. I know it's selfish for me to come running back to you after all of this time. But I now realize that you always been the one for me. I fucked up putting you on the back burner for Mason. I just wanted to make my family work, and look at me. I don't even have custody of my son. My momma refuses to let me see Marcell." I could hear the sadness in her voice.

That was thing with Desi that held me close to her. I always could see the good in her and her potential. When Desi was pregnant, she was so happy about becoming a mother. But she allowed Mason to convince her to do the dumbest shit when it came to Marcell. I was the one who convince Desi to stop fighting her mom for custody of Marcell because of the toxic relationship she and Mason was in. I remember times when Mason wanted to hit a lick so bad he would force Desi to leave Marcell in the house by himself or leave him on her mother's steps. I told her if she loved her son she would allow her mother to take him. I knew if that baby stayed with them he would have died and that would've been a burden that Desi couldn't live with.

"Desi I'm not about to play these games with you. Plus, I don't trust you. That shit you did to Tracey was foul. If you do that shit to somebody who barely knew you existed. I can just imagine what you would do to me."

"Peanut I was young and dumb. So much in my feelings that I didn't feel like what I did was so bad at the time". I looked at this girl like she crazy. Tracey lost five years of her life. She must have noticed my expression because she started to clean up her statement.

"Now I know that I've matured; that was some fucked up shit. I'm trying to change for the better. Get my son and live the best life I can. I know you're the best person to help me become a better me.".

"Desi." I groaned knowing I was about to give in. The look in her eyes made me believe every word she just said.

"Peanut I love you." said admitted and started to unbuckle my pants pulling out my dick. It wasn't long before I was hitting the back of her throat.

"Fuck," I moaned gripping her hair and motioning her to suck faster as I was about to cum.

"Mmmm," Desi swallowed everything I had to offer.

"Peanut I'm serious I want you, and to move on with my life. I moved out of the place me and Mason shared and everything. I got me a room for now at the Marriott downtown."

"Mason knows where you staying."

"Yeah he made an unexpected visit or two trying to force me to do a lick with him. But I'm done with that shit. I know when to bow out gracefully. I know our luck is going to run out one of these days. Plus, starting Monday I'm going to put in some applications to get a real job. I can't get my son back as a stripper."

"Just go to my house and stay there. If we going to make this work I need you safe and away from him." I said pulling my spare key off my key ring.

"Are you sure?" She asked.

"Yeah," I answered, and a huge smile spread across her face. It was like she won the fucking lotto.

"Desi you already know I care for you I always have, but if you think about fucking me over don't forget I know your darkest secret, and the last thing you want to be is on Angelo's hit list. Trust me your death will be a slow and cruel one."

"Peanut I'm not that person anymore. I would never do you dirty." She said before kissing me on the lips.

I'll meet you at my house when I wrap up here."

"Why can't I stay?" Desi asked. I wasn't sure if she was serious or not, but this is the last place she wanted to be. Especially, with GMM swarming around.

"You know this is Tracey's cousin people. Plus, Angelo is here, and I'm not trying to bring beef between my cousin's Law and Aquil and GMM because of you. I'm not Mason; if Angelo fuck with you than I'm going to have to fuck him up."

"I understand just hurry home please. I'm going to get my things out of the room."

"Cool." I kissed her again before we got out the car and started to go our separate ways. She headed to her car, and I headed back over to the kickback to chill with my cousins before I met Desi at my house."

"Where the fuck your go," Law asked as soon I reach them.

"I went to talk to shorty."

"Talk or fuck? Zip ya fucking pants up. I hope you not dumb enough to give that girl the time of day. King just told us she be on some foul shit with her nigga Mason. All I know if some unnecessary heat come my way I'm deading both of y'all. Plus how can you trust a hoe that's sleeping with her husband's best friend." Aquil shook his head. I hated that he thought he knew everything. He was the main reason why it took Law so long to put me on. He kept telling his brother I wasn't fit for this business, and only decided that based off the people I chill with.

"I don't fuck with that nigga anymore and she not with him. Plus me and Desi been had our own relationship for some time now."

"Man keep your eye on that bitch. Her and her nigga already known for jacking people. Don't let pussy blind ya." Law said.

"Yeah ya dumb ass be the on staring down the barrel of that nigga Mason's gun. Niggas like Mason don't like when people are doing better than them. He would love to rob you and kill you for fucking his bitch. That hoe will sit next to him and watch him pull the trigger." Aquil said his piece and walked off with Law following behind him.

I don't give a fuck what they think. Do I trust Desi 100 percent? No. But I know for a fact Desi will never do my dirty; for the simple fact that I hold the information that could have her and anyone she love pushing up Daisys'. Angelo is a undercover sociopath this man along with Pharaoh Black pulled off the Labor Day Massacre in Philadelphia. That Massacre is going down in Philly's history. Everybody knows who did it, but nobody is crazy enough to point the finger; out of fear, their family will be next. Desi will never put herself in that predicament.

"Boy get up!" I heard my father yell with his voice laced with embarrassment. I didn't care I wasn't getting up until I heard their car start and drive out the driveway. As soon as I heard the car wheels burning rubber out of the driveway I decided to get myself together. Ira hit me so hard I knew he probably fractured it. I swear when I catch up with Riley I'm going to beat her ass ten times worse for what the nigga just did to me.

"Dad call the cops!" I said walking up the rest of the driveway only for my father to turn around and walk inside our house.

"Oh, my God! Sebastian, what happen to your face?" My mother cried running over to me.

"I was attacked."

"Attacked! I'm calling the cop where did this happen." My mom moved frantically around the livingroom looking for the house phone to make the call.

"Abigail sit the fuck down somewhere nobody is calling the police." My father snapped causing my mom to stop dead in her tracks. My father may have been a cheating bastard, but he never used that tone of voice with my mother before.

"What happened to him was well deserved. He's out here putting hands on his fiancée like we didn't raise him better."

"So he was attacked because of that girl Riley?" Now my mother was fuming missing the whole point my father was trying to make. She hated Riley so much that she was willing to overlook the fact I was abusing my soon to be wife.

"He's lucky all he got was punch in the face after all of the disgusting and degrading things he did to the girl. I'm surprised she didn't call the cops on him. Now what I want you to do is call off this engagement."

"This is the first thing I've agreed with you on in years." My mother huffed. But not marrying Riley was out of the question.

I loved that girl, and I refuse to have her be with a thug like Ira Black.

"That Riley girl was never of your speed and class. Now Isabella is the person you should have asked to marry you. I think you know that too since you bought her a house, and are sleeping with her every chance you get."

"I'm marrying Riley period," I said with finality. I didn't care what me and Isabella were doing behind Riley's back.

"Son that girl doesn't want you. Accept it, you lost a good woman. Why would she even want to marry you after what you did to her? Multiple trips to the emergency room. You thought it was acceptable to strip her and leave her in the projects to get raped or attacked by some sicko." He reprimanded me. My mother just lowered her head as much as she didn't like Riley she knew I did the unthinkable to that girl.

"I just get so upset with her. It's like I can't control my emotion or actions. I love her, but this is the only way I can show her. I don't want to hurt her. It's just I rather her stay with me out of fear than leave because I messed up a good thing."

"Sebastian you need let go. That little scuffle you encountered outside was just a warning. Riley is mixed up with some dangerous people."

"Riley is mixed up with some dangerous people? I guess we can say the same for you. Why does a well know criminal feel comfortable coming to the house for a chat?"

"What are you trying to say, Sebastian?" My mother asked because my tone of voice was laced with accusations.

"Yeah son if you have something to get off your chest, now is the time and place to do it." My father feared me.

"I just have one question are the rumors floating around about you being a dirty cop and commissioner true?" I knew I just pissed my father off. But I didn't care, he was turning his nose down at me and my relationship. But he has some skeletons in his closet that are coming to light.

"Rumors are just what they are."

"So, your just close friends with the Black family." I chuckled. He was unbelievable lying in my fucking face.

"Sebastian you sitting over there with judgmental eyes like my dealings with the Black family didn't support this livelihood that you and your mother are accustomed too." He said shocking the hell out of me. For the longest, I knew we lived off of my mother's money. With all of the lavish trips we took while I was growing up, I knew my father couldn't afford that off of his salary.

"Keep me out of this." My mother Abigail hissed.

"It's your secrets that are coming to the light."

"Shut the hell up. The money I made on the side kept your drunk ass laced in nothing but gold and diamonds. Don't try to act all high and mighty now. Son how the fuck you think I was able to pay for you to go to Harvard Law education without any financial aid." I look towards my mother waiting for her to put him in his place.

"What you looking at her for? That old money she came from ran out by the time you were five years old. Your mother is not the rich heiress she tries to claim. All of her family's business has been shut down due to the major debt that her father left. So, I did what I had to do and made a deal with the devil himself to make sure my family stayed above water. This is the thanks I get."

I couldn't even say anything because my father was right. Me nor my mother ever wanted for anything. All along my father was putting his job, family, and reputation in jeopardy.

"Sebastian here is some paperwork that you can look over or have another attorney look over. Ira Black has agreed buy you out of the daycares and put everything into Riley's name. The houses and cars Riley and her parents have they are willing to pay for those too." He was out of his mind if he thought I was signing any-thing. Why would I give away my leverage; the only control I have over Riley?

"Tear those papers up, he not signing a damn thing. It was his hard-earned money that opened up those daycares, and it was his money that bought the houses and cars. If Riley wants to move on than she can do so without anything that belongs to my son," My mom snapped. All of my father could do was shake his head.

"At this point I don't give a fuck what you do with the daycares or the properties. Shut them down because you and I both know you're not going to run that business. Regardless if you gave the money to start up the daycares, you know Riley is the reason why they are successful. Plus taking away the houses that you gave to her parents after you basically did everything to convince them to move out of their apartment is messed up. But that's a lesson Riley will have to learn the hard way. I just want you to end what-ever you think y'all have. Those Blacks aren't the one to play with. I have bared witness to some of the most disturbing evil acts a person could encounter because of the Blacks. I just would hate for you to be their next victim."

With that being said he walked away leaving me with my thoughts. I don't know what Riley thought, but she will never be happy without me. Now she has some thugs backing her I was going to take everything she worked for in a blink of an eye.

Chapter 21

Mason

"**W**elcome to Crafty Souls. How can I help you?" The young girl at the counter asked causing me to look up to see who just walked in the restaurant. With Angelo playing mind games lurking in the shadows I couldn't be too careful. It's been weeks, and I was wondering if he ever was going to make his move. I know this was all a game and he wanted me to get comfortable and think all is forgotten before he popped out of the bushes on me. I was waiting for my food when a familiar fragrance invaded my nostrils.

"Yes, my name is Tracey I'm here to pick up the two chicken wing platters," she said

Tracey whipped her head on my direction, and her beauty had me in awe. She was standing in front of me in the simplest outfit ripped boyfriend jeans, white T-shirt and some White Gucci sneaker. Her hair placed in a messy bun at the top of her head and the only make-up she had on was some pink lip gloss. Tracey never had to do much to showcase her beauty. She was so busy smiling in her phone that she didn't even notice me staring a hole through her. Seeing her glowing and smiling just looking happy had me feeling jealous. She was giving her love to somebody else and most likely that person was Angelo. After experiencing love and affection like Tracey's, you'll never want anyone else to experience it.

"Sir!" The girl at the counter called out to me letting me knows that my order was ready. Walking up to the counter I could feel Tracey's eyes burning a hole through me. It's sad that there's so much hate and resentment that she holds against me. But she has every right to feel the way she does.

"Is this her food?" I asked the girl.

"Yes," she said with an attitude. She has been trying to flirt with me since I ordered my food.

"Here this should cover everything," I said handing her fifty.

"You can keep the change?"

"I can pay for my food Mason." Tracey hissed snatching her bag off the counter and tossed her money at me before walking out of the restaurant.

Picking up her money and grabbing my food I quickly chased after her. Looking around I seen her walking across the street unlocking her Mercedes G Wagon.

"*Damn!*" I muttered shorty was doing better than I thought.

"Tracey," I called her name dodging traffic trying to get to her before she pulled off. By time I got to her, she was already starting her car. Knocking on her window, she unrolled her window.

"Wassup stranger?"

"Mason what the fuck do you want." Tracey snapped. Looking in her eyes I felt like shit for doing what I did to her. I could never give her those years back and who knows what she endured in my absence.

"Tracey, I know I'm the worse person in the world to you right now. And I know I caused you a lot of pain..."

"Why Mason? Why would you do me like that? I ruined my life for you. I had goal and dreams, and I put everything off because I wanted to save you from imprisonment." She yelled. I could see the tears forming in her eyes.

"Mason I was pregnant with our child, and you abandoned me."

"Where's the child now? I asked the question that I never wanted to ask. I never truly wanted to know what happended to me and Tracey's child. With me not having knowledge of him/her; it help me to never feel guilty for my choices. With my son Marcell, I feel guilty for not being in his life because I know the feeling of being abandoned by my parents. But Marcell is in better hands with Desi's mom taking care of him

"I had a miscarriage." The hurt and sadness was evident in her voice. As crazy as this may sound I was slightly hoping she had the baby, so I could have some connection to her.

I'm sorry Tracey." I muttered with my head hanging low.

"There's no excuse for what I did. I was scared I had no clue on how I could take care of a child by myself."

"Yet you decided to get that bitch Desi pregnant and marry the hoe."

"I married her out of convenience. She was always talking about snitching and shit. Me messing with Desi was the last thing I should have done. When I found out she sent you that bullshit in the mail, I fucked her up. As for my son, Marcell doesn't even know me. I'm the last person who needs to be anybody's father. We lost custody of him to Desi's mother after he was two month's old."

"Man it is what it is. It was a lesson learned for me." She muttered. I knew I was being optimistic with this next question that I was about to ask. But I didn't want this to be our last conversation. I just wanted to make things right. I know we will never be what we were, but if I can get her to stop hating me, I will take that over anything.

"Let me get your number. I know you have more things to get off of your chest. I have so much I want to say to you too. Maybe I can take you out to dinner or something."

Tracey looked at me like I lost my damn mind it was like a switch went off in her head. Her once tense face relaxed, and she surprised me when she took out her phone and gave it to me. I placed my number in it and texted myself so I could have her number.

"I'm going to hit you up later," I said before walking to my car, and she pulled off.

I headed straight to my house I shared with Desi. As of lately, she been spending all of her time with Peanut trying to gain his trust. I knew Peanut damn near all my life, and once that nigga is in love, he will pillow talk like a muthafucka. For real I don't even want the guns that he sale. I'm just going to rob him blind of his profit than get ghost. Desi already told me his cousin's Law and Aquil didn't like her and feel like she was scheming. The last thing I need is another crazy nigga like Aquil gunning for me.

I just pulled up to house, and I looked at my phone. I still couldn't believe Tracey gave me her number. A part of me wanted to think she gave in too easily and it was probably a setup. But another part of me knew that wasn't Tracey's character. Getting out of the car I looked around at my surroundings to see if anything was out of the ordinary and it wasn't. That was until a white van pulled up and its tires screeched. The driver pressed on the breaks to stop in front of my house. My heart rate increased as I watched three masked men jump out of the back of the van in all black. I don't know why I couldn't move; it was like I was paralyzed with fear. It wasn't until they were like five steps away from me before my feet allowed me to try and run towards my house.

"Where the fuck ya bitch ass running too?" A deep voice boomed before I was hit in the head with something making everything go black.

I don't know how long I've been knocked out, but I woke up sitting at a round table with five other people who all look scared out of their mind. My head was pounding, and my vision was a little blurry. Shaking my head, I tried to get myself together. Nobody was tied up, so I didn't understand why nobody to escaped. We looked to be in some type of cabin.

me. All I could do was curled into the fetal position to block the blows.

"Alright y'all I didn't want yall to kill his bitch ass," Angelo stated, and the beating stopped.

"Damn!" Cream mouth hung open. I could only see out of one good eye.

"I promised ya brother that I would allow you to live when he called and beg for your life. He all out of favors and I don't give a fuck who best friend he is. If you keep fucking with me and my team, it lights out." Angelo said snatching my right arm and laid it in front of me. I was too weak to move or do anything. I knew I had multiple broken bones.

"Ahhhhhhh!" I screamed as I felt my right hand get cut off. I was losing blood quickly.

"That's for trying to take from GMM muthafucka," Angelo whispered in my ear.

"Wrap his hand up then drop his bitch ass in the parking lot of the closest hospital." Was the last thing I heard before I faded into the darkness.

Chapter 22

Blue

Three Months Later....

Today was one of those days that I didn't want to be bothered. Today was no other than the anniversary of my nigga Sean's death. Even though I killed Ross years ago, Sean's death still bothers me. I just got off the phone with my sis Reign and she taking it as she always does. No matter many years have gone by things have never been the same without the homie. Reign sounded depressed, and Angelo hasn't answered his phone. I wasn't so worried about Reign her fiancée can take care of her. It was her birthday, so I know he planned something decent for her to keep her mind off the past.

But Angelo hot-headed ass is the one who's going to stress me out. Around this time, he's liable to get in trouble. Angelo had some unresolved issues within himself. He thinks I'm playing when I tell him talk to a therapist, but he truly needs professional help. Angelo holds the guilt of Sean's murder over his head just like I do. Ross killed Sean to get back at Angelo and Cream for robbing his little brother Lyle of his shipment. The only reason why Angelo and Cream robbed Lyle was because Lyle jumped Cream with his friend, because Cream fucked his baby mama. When Sean learned that Ross was searching for Angelo and Cream, we went on our own manhunt and beat Ross damn near to death.

I always told Sean we should have just killed him. A nigga like Ross would never take that lying down. Ross laid low for a few months. Then on Reign's twentieth birthday Sean was throwing her this big birthday bash. Everybody was coming out to party

"What the fuck are you talking about. Nobody set Mason up." Pookie hissed. There was some people around, and the last thing he wanted was word to get out that he was a snitch. It was bad enough there were rumors and everyday he pays for those rumors by fighting to protect himself.

"So, you got amnesia." Mike snapped before punching Pookie in the face. Mike had handsand mix with his bad temper things could turn deadly. After a couple combinations, Mike finally landed Pookie on his ass, and started stomping him out. Mike kicked him a couple more times before he pulled out a shank.

"Aye chill the fuck out!" I couldn't allow Mike a commit another murder he was too close to getting out. Me I have life with no chance of parole.

"Naw fuck him. He got Mason beefing with muthafuckas because of his snake ass."

"I didn't set up Mason," Pookie said before spitting out blood from his mouth. Mike went to charge after him again, but I stop him. I wanted to hear the truth.

"Why would I set my cousin baby daddy up. Your brother had my cousin making the drops. Why would I put Desi's life on the line like that? When I got knocked,Desi came to visit me. I told her what was up and told them to cease all contact with the connect. Next thing I know your brother sent his other bitch Tracey to make the drop. Knowing damn well she was meeting with the cops. If anybody's a snake its ya bitch ass brother."

Rage filled my body. Pookie made some valid points. He's probably not telling the whole truth, but he is telling the truth about giving them the heads up. Like he said what would he have to gain from getting his cousin locked up. If Mason knew he about the undercover he probably didn't believe him. Tracey was like a little sister to me too. I was mad when she took the bid for Mason, but now hearing he set her up on purpose had me wanting to snap. You already know when I get in contact with Lo, Mason is as good as dead. All these years we tried to give him the benefit of the doubt.

"I asked Desi why he send that girl knowing the cops was the so-called connect. Desi told me it was get back at some nigga named Angelo."

My eyes darted to Mike, and his face was unreadable as he stood there in silence.

"Your fucking brother is as good as dead," I muttered before Mike turned around and stabbed me in the chest with the shank. My eyes bulge out of my head in shock.

"What.... the fuck.... Mike." I mumble as I felt the shank stab me a couple more times all over my upper body.

"I'm sorry Blue. I can't allow this to get back to Lo. Blood over everything." He then turn to chased after Pookie who was too shocked to move and stabbed him in the neck. Then he ran out of the library. Never would I have thought I would die at the hand of a nigga I feed, my best fucking friend, the person who I would kill for. As I faded to the light the only thought I had was baby girl Blu at least the last words I told her was I love her.

Chapter 23

Naomi

"Girl I'm starving," Lala stressed as we walked into her favorite restaurant Green Eggs Café.

"Well, we're here now," I said with an agitated tone causing her to cock her head to the side.

"Naomi stops acting like that. I'm treating you to breakfast to get you out of your damn house. The least you could do is show some interest instead of acting like I'm holding you hostage." Lala snapped making me feel bad instantly. All she was trying to do was get me out of the funk I been in lately.

Ever since that dreadful night three months ago Angelo literally cut me off. I haven't been myself. I never been lovesick before, but I can barely function at work, and all I do is sit in the house and be depressed. I tried multiple times to reach out to him but never received an answered. The last time I called, it said the number was no longer in service. I felt like a stalker digging up his old information I had on him while he was on parole. But was to no use since he move from the apartment that he was living in as soon as I signed my signature on the dotted line freeing him from parole. It so sad that I loved a man I barely even knew. Come to think about it he never took me to his new place. I never met any of his friends or family. I guess I was nothing but a nut to him. That's what hurt me the most.

"Lala I'm sorry. I just have been really messed up these past couple months. I truly love him. I'm not ready to move on. I hate that you set this little double date up with Samuel and Elijah," I said before the hostess told us to follow her to the table.

"Sis I know you did but its time to move on. Plus ..." Lala started but stop dead in her tracks, and I didn't know why because the hostess was continuing on to two tables behind the one we are standing next to.

"Good Morning can we help you." A female voice asked in a pleasant tone. A voice that brought my attention to the table we were standing next to, and my heart literally broke in a thousand pieces. Sitting at the table was no other than the man I wish would give me the time of day.

"Good Morning," Lala spoke to the girl. It wasn't her who she had the problem with. Angelo eyes darted pass my sister and landed on me. His intense stare made me feel uncomfortable; his face held no emotion.

"Wassup Naomi and Lala." He finally spoke.

I had so many emotions swarming my body a part of me wanted to ask to speak with him alone. Another part wanted me to snap and ask who this bitch was sitting across from him. Here I am thinking about him day in and day out, and it seems like I could be the last thing on his mind.

"Y'all know each other." The girl asked looking back and forth between me and Lala and Angelo.

"Yeah..." I answered before he cut me off.

"Yeah, we were old friends. Naomi this is Tracey, Tracey this Naomi and her pit-bull looking ass sister Lala."

My words got caught in my throat as I stared at the famous Tracey. The girl who stole his heart and refuses to let it go. She was beautiful more beautiful than I thought she would be. All I knew was that she was his teenage love and he lost her. But I guess they found one another because here she was in the flesh. Looking at her caused me to become self-conscious of myself as my hands started to mess with my clothes.

"Nice meeting you ladies," Tracey smirked catching on quickly that one of us use to mess with Angelo. Even though she didn't let on, I could tell she was bothered and probably had multiple thoughts running through her head. I knew I would. I hated that Lala made our presence known. Now I wanted to walk out of the restaurant and go home.

"Nice meeting you too," I muttered.

"Good seeing y'all enjoy y'all brunch." Angelo dismissed us without even looking back in our direction. Instead, he grabbed Tracey hand bringing her attention back to him so they could continue to enjoy their meal.

"Tracey it was nice meeting you too. Angelo, I hope you treat her way better than you did my sister." Lala hissed embarrassing the hell out of me. Why did she have to go there? I wasn't about to show my ass in this restaurant.

"I'm pretty sure he already does." Tracey simply said with a wink and a smirk that I wanted to slap off. But how could I when Lala came to them starting shit. Plus, I know she's not lying. I was jealous of Tracey when she was just a figment of my imagination. Now staring at her I was green with envy like never before.

"Lala, I don't know what you call yourself doing, but you about to make me embarrass the shit out you and ya sister. Naomi knew what it was. Now if she took it upon herself to think more into the situation that's her problem. I advise you to get to the table with those gentlemen who been grilling the fuck out of me before all four of y'all come up missing." He said looking at Lala whose eyes was bulging out of her head by his threat that I wasn't taking lightly.

"Sorry for the disruption. Go back to enjoying your meal." I said pulling Lala in the direction of her husband Samuel, and his best friend, Elijah.

"Is everything okay?" Elijah asked as soon as we hit the table.

"Yeah who was that Lala?" Samuel wanted to know giving Lala the side eyes. Ever since his secret child and baby mama popped up, he knew Lala was going to step out on him. All I could do was shake my head at his subliminal accusation. Little did Samuel know Lala loved him and would never cheat on him. Sometimes I think he wants her to cheat so he can call them even. What he doesn't realize is even if she cheats, he's the one with the constant reminder of his infidelities.

"Don't start Sam," Lala said rolling her eyes.

"That was no one important. Hey Elijah, and yes we are okay."

"How have you been Naomi." Elijah started the conversation between us.

"I'm good. Are y'all ready to order I'm starving." I said trying to enjoy this unwanted double date.

Throughout brunch, Elijah, Lala, and Samuel did most of the talking. I could barely focus on what going on at my table because all of my attention was staring at Angelo. It's a damn shame the way I wanted this man. Besides his good looks, he was street and book smart. He wasn't a square like Elijah here. I knew if some shit went down I didn't have to worry. Looking at Tracey, she was all smiles just like I knew she would be. She's fucking Angelo Hart. That dick would put a smile on a nuns face. I thought they probably wouldn't enjoy the rest of their meal with the little show that Lala put on, but they looked like long lost lovers. However, there was a look of sadness in his eyes that I couldn't quite put my finger on. Then it hit me today was the day of his brother's death.

Watching Tracey head to the bathroom, I made my move. "I'll be right back."

I quickly walked back over to Angelo's table, and I could feel Lala's eyes burning a hole in my back. I already knew I was about to hear an earful once we were alone. She didn't understand that I loved this man probably the way she loved her dog ass husband.

It's obvious he moved on, and I wasn't one to step on anybody toes I just wanted him to know that I will always be here for him if he needs me. Just last year I was the one who's shoulder he was leaning on during this time.

"What do you want Naomi?" Angelo asked as if my presence bothered him. Then had the nerve to look over his shoulder towards the women's bathroom.

"I'm not coming over here to start any trouble. I wanted to come back over here to apologize about Lala. She had no right coming for you the way she did. Plus, I know what today is, and the last thing you need is drama. So, if you ever need me you know my number and my address don't be afraid to use it." I leaned down and gave him a hug that he didn't reject then took the chance and kissing him on his neck.

"Thanks, Naomi." He said before drinking the rest of his orange juice. I took that as my hint to walk away.

"Is everything okay?" Elijah asked with a look of annoyance on his face. I couldn't even blame him I wasn't much of a date. Here he trying to entertain me, and I was worried about the next nigga.

"Yeah, he was just an old friend. This is the anniversary of his brother's death. I just wanted to make sure he was okay." I answered avoiding everybody's eyes and continued to eat my food. The rest of brunch was a blur as I continued to watch Angelo and Tracey until they left.

"Can I get you guys anything else?" The waitress asked.

"No thanks, just the check," Samuel answered for everybody.

"The bill has been paid for by the gentleman that was sitting at the other table." She said before walking away leaving everybody with shocked looks on their face. I pulled out my vibrating cell phone and had a text from an unknown number.

Unknown Number: *Thanks for making sure I was good. Enjoy brunch on me. Lo*

188

Chapter 24

Angelo

Walking to the car I knew Tracey had an attitude. Even though we stayed and enjoyed the rest of our meal. I knew she was upset about the whole situation with Naomi and Lala. When they walked away, her whole mood and vibe changed, and I hated that she let some irrelevant females piss her off.

"Naomi was way before me, and you made it official," I said addressing the purple elephant in the room before she started making any more assumptions. Driving off I glanced over at her, and I could see the irritation covering her face.

"Angelo, I didn't even say anything." Tracey nonchalantly shrugged.

"Tracey, I know you. Even though you didn't voice what you're thinking. I know you have crazy thoughts and assumption running through ya head. I'm clearing up any doubt you may have."

"How long ago was it Lo? Because that girl looked heartbroken and don't think I didn't notice that her weird ass was burning a hole through my back while we continued our date. What's the story between y'all?"

I sighed getting annoyed myself because I knew Tracey was insecure due to her past relationship. Even because of how our situation ended. So, I knew I had to be understanding. I just hope she didn't start acting insecure about her position in my life because that's one way of making our relationship not work.

"It's nothing much. She was my parole officer. I was fucking here and there. Someway somehow you caught feelings, and I deaded the shit when she thought she could be more to me." I answered honestly. I never been one to lie.

"The sister seems more upset than ya old bitch. Did you fuck her too?" Tracey snapped. There it was I wanted to laugh in her damn face. Tracey's jealousy was out of this world. I'm surprised she didn't snap sooner and get us kicked out.

"Hell, naw I didn't fuck that damn troll. She just hates the situation me and her sister had going on."

"Hmmm." Tracey sat back, and she rolled her eyes.

"Angelo don't get fucked up. I'm not about to go through the same shit I did with Mason with you with the secret side bitches.

She pissed me off comparing me to the ass bitch nigga. Little did Tracey know she was basically the side bitch turn main bitch. Desi has been around way longer that she could imagine.

"Naw don't you get fuck up bringing that fuck nigga name up in my presence. Don't even compare me to him. If I wanted to fuck other bitches I wouldn't make shit official with you. I didn't even play those games with you as a youngbul."

"Angelo I wasn't trying to upset you." Tracey started but she already pushed me over the edge.

"Naw you pissed me the fuck off. You knew what you were doing when you let the words slip right out of ya mouth. Now you're looking dumb. I already told you about the insecurities and shit. I'm not paying for another nigga's mistakes."

"Another nigga's mistakes?" she asked. Looking at me like I was the one in the wrong.

"If I'm not mistaken ain't you the one who had a whole bitch visiting you up in jail while we were together."

"You know damn well we weren't together."

"Nigga you took my virginity and was cock-blocking like a muthafucka so yeah we were together. Fuck you mean! A nigga couldn't even look at me without you going bat shit crazy." Tracey stated nothing but facts.

"Whatever... The fact still remains that you wasn't my girl. Plus, the hoe was nothing but a drug mule. I wasn't claiming that dumb bitch she was out here trafficking drugs for a nigga that wouldn't give her the time of day outside of jail. Risking her life because I told her what she wanted to hear."

"If that's how you feel I guess I'm a dumb hoe too."

"Man take that shit how you want... But don't compare me to some nigga who did you dirty and had you so far gone in the fucking head. He had you playing side bitch to his main hoe. Desi been around way longer," I snapped pulling up to her job. As soon as the words left my lips, I felt bad because I knew my anger wasn't because of her comparing me to Mason. This was the anniversary of Sean death. It never failsevery year around this time I'm not myself. I would think that the guilt I felt for my brother dying would have diminished over the years, but it hasn't. It just seems like I only get angrier and angrier. Blue often tells me I should go to see a therapist. But that wasn't me. I always been one to work out my own problems.

"Angelo I'm going to act like this argument never happen." She said pointing between the both of us.

"I know what today is. That's the reason why I went out of my way to get you out of the house and do something special. I know you hurt and hurt people hurt people. No need to come pick me up I'll catch a ride home. Just hit me up when you get out of this negative funk you're in."

With that said Tracey got out and slammed my door shut before walking into Reign's Day Spa. Was I going to go after her? No,

"Wassup shorty."

"Nothing I just wanted to make sure you were okay," Naomi said.

"I'm good. I'm drunk as shit probably shouldn't even be driving." I admitted.

"Please be careful Angelo."

"I will," I said before my phone died on her. Now I was pissed because I wasn't able to look up her address. Pulling off my destination was to go back to my condo, but for some reason, I ended up standing in front of Naomi's door knocking.

"Angelo…" Naomi said my name confusedly.

"What are you doing here?"

"Man, I honestly don't know," I answered swaying a little to the side.

"I need you to release some of this pent-up aggression." My man stiffened taking in Naomi's appearance dressed in nothing but a silk robe.

"Come in." There was nothing else needed to be said as I walked into her house and ended up in her bedroom.

Chapter 25

Ira

"Look who showed up for Sunday dinner." My Aunt Maria announced as soon as me, Riley, and Troi walked through the front door.

I knew my presence would be a surprise. I haven't really shown up for Sunday dinner in a while. Honestly, I never really started coming since me, and Amelia stopped years ago. It wasn't that I didn't want to come because I always enjoyed spending time with my family. Just been so busy with my own life to do so. Ms. Ella finally told me that she has stage four lung cancer. Finding out about her illness had me feeling down. But I knew I had to be strong not only for Troi but for her. I'm was optimistic, and I was putting all my faith into God. I wasn't claiming death because that wasn't an option. Ms. Ella's always been strong. So, I made sure I was at every one of her doctor's appointments. Also, I gave her the best doctor's that money could buy.

"And he brought company," Queen said with a warm smile bringing everybody's attention to Riley, who was standing behind me shyly. I had to admit the women in my family were kind of intimidating.

"Hey, Riley," Reign smile waving her over to where they were all sitting in the kitchen.

"You must be special if he's bringing you to Sunday dinner." My Aunt Maria said before telling Riley to sit next to her. I already knew she was about to grill her. I smiled as Riley looked nervous. Her ass begged me not to leave her with my aunt and cousins.

"Aunt Maria be nice," I asked causing everybody to laugh.

"Ira." She gasped with her hand over her chests to say how dare I.

"I will. I just want to get a feel for her. You know you always been my favorite. I can tell you feeling her because you have the same look on ya face when you was with Amelia." My Aunt read me like an open book. I was really feeling Riley. We haven't done anything sexually, but I was slowly falling for the person she's turning out to be. Not only was she just this awesome person. The bond her and Troi share is a bond I don't want to end. Troi finally feels like she has a mother figure in her life. At her Summer camp, they were holding a tea party for the mother and daughters, and she was beyond excited to ask Riley to go with her.

"Really mom." Queen shook her head still stuck on the favorite part, but what Mama Maria said was true. I was her favorite. I think she felt she needed to love me extra because I lost both parents at a young age.

"Shut up Queen. You had Royal wrapped around your boney finger since your unexpected ass popped out of the coochie." My Aunt and Uncle always tell the story about how she was in labor to deliver King and the doctor shocked them when she said she had another baby to push out. It's crazy because that's the same thing that happen to Pharaoh fiancée Reign.

"On that note, I'm headed down to the den," I said before walking over to the stove and snatching a piece of fried chicken.

"So, Riley is it...." I chuckled walking down the steps to my Uncle's man cave. This is where all of the men stayed while the woman prepared dinner.

"Look what the wind-blown in," Pharaoh announced. He was the first person to see me coming down.

"Wassup Nephew." Uncle Royal stood up and gave me a hug, and I dapped everybody else up. Downstairs was Pharaoh, King,

Majesty, Teddy, and Kelz. They were already smoking and drinking as they do at every Sunday dinner.

"Nothing just stacking my bread. Me, Angelo, and Cream about to open up a couple of gas stations, car washes, and laundry mats."

"That's good to hear." Royal approved before walking upstairs.

"That's good to hear. Y'all bringing in too much money not to have some legit business to wash y'all money." Pharaoh said.

"I know... Kelz you think you can find us some properties to start the businesses on."

"Yeah, that's not going to be a problem," Kelz said smoking on his Cuban Cigar.

"Who that pretty young thing ya aunt in there interrogating." Royal laughed looking at me. I know Riley is going to kill me leaving her with them.

"That's Riley."

"Why you leave her up there with ya Aunt. You know she about to have somebody run a background check on her and her family." Royal chuckled because his wife was crazy and didn't trust anyone.

"How's the whole thing going with the commissioner's Son; is he still a problem," Pharaoh asked.

"I don't understand why y'all just don't let me end his life." I let out a breath of frustration.

Sebastian was the worst type of nigga you could deal with. He was weak and always had to be in control. Riley standing on her own two feet was killing him. He was doing everything to break her and have her running back. After numerous fail attempts of him calling and texting he was sorry and begging for her to come back and give their relationship another try. He decided to go the extra mile and started shutting down the daycares. Not caring that his selfish decisions making was not only hurting Riley but the parents of the children who attended the daycare and his employees.

"You just can't kill him things are complicated. Is he still messing with Riley?" Royal asked.

"Not physically. He's been trying to contact her, and since that didn't work, he shut down all the daycares. Sebastian hasn't signed the documents allowing me to buy all of the daycares, her house, and her parents' house from him."

"He's not," King said shaking his head.

"Yeah, those business and properties is the only leverage that he had over Riley. He's going to use them to best of his abilities. Riley just may need to chalk that shit up as a lesson learned in doing bad business." Majesty said, and I knew he was probably right. The problem that I have is that he's not going to stop at the daycares. I know it was only a matter of time before he started fucking with her parents.

"Dinner." One of the ladies yelled downstairs to the den.

As we all made our way to the dining room, Tori said grace for the family and everybody dug in. Riley was all smiles interacting with my family. Looking around the room, I could see everybody was loving her vibe and that was good. Everybody talked and joke about everything under the sun it was ten o'clock when people started to make theie way out the house.

"Cousin Ira," Jamie said walking up to me and King with Troi right behind her.

"Ahh hell naw," King muttered as they both put on their puppy dog faces trying to butter us up.

"Can Troi spend the night at my house. I already asked my mommy, and she said yes and will take us to camp in the morning. Now all you have to do is say yes." Jamie said all in one breath.

"Please!" Troi begged looking up at me with brown doe eyes.

"Sure," I said with a smirk. This little girl can get me to say yes to anything.

"Yay! Daddy, you have to take us to the store to get all of the snacks." Jamie said to King who just shook his head. She had him wrapped around her little finger too.

"Whatever you say baby girl it's your world." King chuckled as they started to get ready to leave.

"You ready," I said in Riley's ear. She was talking to my Aunt Maria, and Reign still sipping on some champagne.

"Umm yeah... where's Troi."

"She suckered me into allowing her to spend the night with Tempest and King."

"Oh okay."

"Riley it was so nice meeting you. I hope to see at the next Sunday dinner." Aunt Maria said giving her a hug and nodded her head in approval to me.

"See y'all later," I said before walking out if their front door.

The whole ride back to my house she was telling me how much she enjoyed my family and loved my Aunt Maria even though she subliminally threatened her. All I could do was laugh because my Aunt Maria was crazy about the men in her family. That's one person whose bad side you didn't want to get on. As soon as we got into the house, I headed straight to the shower allowing the water beads to massage my body. The shower door slide open. Standing in front of me was Riley just as naked as the day he was born.

"Can I join you." She asked not really waiting for a response as she stepped inside. My eyes observed her body as the water cascaded over her body. Her body was nothing short of perfection. Stepping into her personal space I couldn't resist, but to pull her into my arms. Riley dived in with a kiss wrapping her arm around my neck. Picking her up she wrapped her legs around my waist. I

Chapter 26

Riley

"Ahhhh, Ira!" I screamed feeling myself cum on his chocolate dick. I swear I was in heaven.

"Damn ma," Ira groaned through gritted teeth. Gripping my hips as I countiuned to ride the wave he had my body experiencing.

Sex with him was so amazing. After experiencing Ira, I don't know what the hell Sebastian called himself doing. I swear this man woke up every nerve in my body. I love everything about him from his chocolate skin to the curve in his dick that's guaranteed to hit my spot with every stroke, to his mean but caring personality.

"You riding... the shit out this dick." He moaned slapping my ass causing me to bounce up and down faster and harder.

"Shhhhhh..." Ira was sending me over the edge as he thrust his hips upward pounding inside of my love.

"Mmmm hmm you about to cum." He muttered as I felt myself reaching my peak. With a few more strokes my juices were pouring down as my pussy causing him cum shortly after.

"I love you." I blurted out coming off my orgasmic high. I didn't even realize what I had just said until I saw the look of anger and disappointment on his face. It was the truth, and now I was embarrassed. Ira silently slide from under me and headed straight to the shower.   His reaction to my confession hurt my feelings; I can't lie. I know he's never gotten over Tori's mother Amelia, but damn was I truly competing with a ghost. I never expected him to forget her or the love they once shared, but I needed him to give me all of him.

I could be jumping the gun because our relationship status was never sat in stone. But here I am month's later living with this man and helping raise Troi and help with Ms. Ella's care while she's going through chemo. Ira seems to never been one talk about his feelings, but he could handle me more carefully.

Getting up I went to use the other bathroom. I was going to my parents' house today. I haven't been around them lately because I didn't want to explain the chaos that was going on in my life. While showering, I came to the decision it was probably time for me to get myself together and move on my own. As much as I hate to admit it, I became emotionally, physically, and financially dependent on Ira. I could see this was becoming the same cycle that I was in with Sebastian. Everything I have now can be ripped away from me. I didn't want to go back to the house. Sebastian bought me, but I think I should stay there until I get back on my feet. Walking into the guest room where I was staying in the beginning. Ira was sitting on the bed fully dressed.

"Riley...." he started, but I quickly cut him off. I didn't need any excuses or his sympathy. I didn't want him to feel the need to say something that he didn't mean.

"Ira just act like I didn't say anything. It's not that serious I was caught up in the moment." I lied trying to save face.

"Act like you didn't say anything?" he hissed. Now I was confused when I admitted my love to him, he looked pissed like I just ruined the moment. Now he's mad because I'm telling him to act like the shit didn't happen.

"Riley you on some bullshit," Ira said shaking his before walking out of the room and the front door. See what I mean he's confusing. I just got myself ready and headed over to my parents' house. Walking up the steps to the house I hated that their stabil-

Kissing him. The blatant disrespect you displayed. Then you call yourself moving out of our home and moving in with him."

"Riley who is this man?" My dad hated the idea of shaking up. He hated the fact that I decided to move in with Sebastian before we were actually married.

"Sebastian you throwing out my dirt, but do you realized the same incident you're talking about you were with ya whore of a secretary that you been fucking for God knows how long." I snapped ignoring my father's question. At this moment Ira was irrelevant.

"Not only where you unfaithful, you been putting your hands on me ever since we've been engaged."

"What!." My father barked charging towards Sebastian only for me to stand in front of him. As much I would have loved to see my daddy put an old school beat down on Sebastian. I don't want that ass whopping to be the reason why they are homeless.

"Wait a minute Sebastian you didn't tell me that." My mother said looking like a Chuckie doll; as she turned her head to look at Sebastian. He had a look of surprise mixed with anger because I let the cat out of the bag.

"Riley how many times I have to apologize. I promise that I will never do that again." Sebastian said as his voice cracked. I know he wasn't about to cry.

"Listen maybe y'all should go to counseling." My mother tried to reason.

"No Sebastian did things to me that I could never forgive or overlook. I say we should just cut our loses." I said letting every-body know this relationship was over.

"Riley get your bag we're going home. I'm tired of these she-nanigans that you are playing." Sebastian yelled looking at me with his cold eyes causing a chill to run down my spine.

"She ain't going anywhere." My dad said getting in Sebastian personal space.

"If you don't bring ya ass home. You and parents can kiss everything goodbye the houses and the cars."

"Nigga we don't need that." My dad snapped gripping Sebastian up by collar of his suite jacket and cocking his fist back to punch him in the face. My mother and I rushed over to them to stop the fight before it started.

"If she don't come ya wife will go to jail," Sebastian muttered but everybody could him clearly. The room became so quite I swear you could hear a mouse piss on cotton. Looking at my mother she had tears instantly coming to her eyes. My father let Sebastian go and turned his attention, my mother.

"What is he talking about Virginia?"

"I never meant to do it. It was an accident." My mother cried out.

"What is going on?"

"Remember the Leah Lambert hit and run," Sebastian said with a smile and my mother looked to be having a nervous breakdown.

"Virginia ..."

I was in total shock. The Leah Lambert story rocked the city of Philadelphia. Leah was an eight-year little girl who was hit walking to school with her little. Leah's body flew fifty feet in the air before her body came crashing down to the ground. This happen four years ago the same time my mother decided to stop drinking. As low key as it was kept my mother was a full-blown alcoholic. It gotten so bad that my father threatened to divorce her if she didn't get her act together. I always thought she changed because of her family. Not because she killed an innocent child. Leah's case had run cold, and nobody could understand how the person was never caught because it happen in broad daylight.

"Ralph I'm so sorry. I will never forgive myself for that accident." My mother fell in my father arms crying. Now everything made sense. Sebastian out of nowhere brought my mother a new car without a problem.

"Just like I made that disappear I can bring it back up. You wouldn't be able to survive jail. I will make sure they will throw you in jail and throw away the key."

"You will incriminate yourself," I shouted

"Riley you know I'm smarter than that. I had ya mom bring it to a junkyard which is now abandon the car is still there untouched. I'm pretty sure the forensic scientist can find poor little Leah's blood on the car. I also have her confession recorded. That alone will be all of the evidence I need. Now all of this could be swept back under the rug if you come home and marry me."

"Like hell, she will marry you." My father roared.

"Then Virginia get ready for ya three hots and cot." Sebastian laughed my family was falling apart in front of me.

"Riley please just go with him." My mother beg causing my father to give her the death stare.

"How dare you ask her to go to the man that been abusing her? Are you fucking serious! You really want our daughter to sacrifice her happiness and life for your own."

"I'm sorry, I can't go to jail."

I didn't want to see my mother in jail either. Even though it hurt me for her to just trade me to the devil himself. The tears began to fall as I realized my life was going to be filled with misery and it was no escaping.

"Okay," I muttered causing my father to storm out of the house without looking back.

"Only under certain conditions."

"Baby you really don't have any ground to make demands in the situation. But I'll hear you out."

"The beatings have to stop. Once we are married, I want all of the daycares, me and my parent's house all in my name. I want the deed to everything, so you could never had this shit over my head again." I demanded still in disbelief. The man I once loved was totally blackmailing me to be with him.

"I'll give you everything you want. Just know there's no divorce. We're in this till death do us part. Just so you don't get cold feet. I hired a wedding planner to plan the wedding we're getting married in three months."

"What!" He was out of him mind.

"I'm not going to change my mind you are holding a murder over my mother's head."

"We're doing things my way so if I say we're getting married in three months then that's what we're doing. Now I suggest you call a tow truck to tow ya little boyfriend car to his house." I forgot I'd been driving Ira's Bentley around ever since the night Sebastian kicked me out of the car naked

"Baby please just do whatever he says." My mom said with tears in her eyes. But mine had nothing but resentment as they pierced through her.

"Let's go home." Sebastian reached out to grab my hand only for me to snatch it away. I stormed out of the house and to his car. I could hear my mother crying in the distance. I don't even know where my father and I don't even know if he and my mother can survive this shit. I wanted to be mad at her, but at the end of the day I fell for a man like Sebastian; now I have to do everything in my power to keep my parents safe and not homeless. The whole ride to our destination my tears wouldn't stop falling. Mainly because of Troi. I hated that I would now just up disappear out of her life.

"We're here," Sebastian announced bringing me out of the daze. Looking up we wasn't standing in front of the house we once shared. We was sitting in a driveway was of a Victorian style house.

"Whose house is that?" I asked as we both got out of the car.

"Ours. I wanted us to have a fresh start. Six bedrooms four bathrooms. I upgraded your car which is in the garage..." Sebastian continued raving about our new house, and all I could do was think how I was about to be held hostage in something so beautiful.

"Riley, did you hear me?"

"Umm no, what did you say," I asked as we started walking towards the front door.

"I said are you ready to see the inside of the h...." he said before he was cut off by the front door swinging open.

"Baby I thought that was you." Isabella walked out the house with a smile on her face that was soon wiped off when she spotted me.

"What the hell is she doing here? Isabella hissed. I couldn't even respond because my eyes was glued to her protruding belly.

This bitch is pregnant!

Chapter 27

Tracey

It's been a couple days since our girls outing and Mason blew up my spot in front of everybody. I understood what my girls were saying about me playing with fire. I feel as though nobody can speak on my situation. I didn't want to involve anyone in my get back plan. Everybody didn't get hurt by Mason's deceit. I'm the only one who experienced the pain of losing five years of her life for a man she loved and thought he loved her. Mason had been blowing my phone up being annoying as hell. When we went to dinner all he talked about was how much in love he was with me and if he could turn back the hands of time, he would. Basically, wanting me to kill him even more. I don't think anyone realized that I would'nt not be able to move forward until he suffered like I did. The only reason why I've been falling back from my little mission is because me and Angelo haven't been on the best of terms.

Angelo been real distant and short with me and it was beginning to bother me. I felt like I was losing him. I call he barely answers, and he only texts back with one-word answers. I felt like he was still in one of his moods because of the annive\

rsary of Sean's death. It wasn't until I found my iPad screen shattered and the screen was frozen on my text messages from Mason. I was pissed at myself for having my phone and iPad connected where my iMessage would come through onto my iPad. However, I was thankful I was smart enough to erase the messages, so the only one he saw was Mason thanking me for going out to dinner. So here I am banging on his front door.

"Tracey, what fuck you doing here?" He barked after snatching open his door with one hand while holding his gun with the other. Standing in nothing but a pair of boxers

"What the hell you mean why I'm here?" Like was he serious? I stormed inside looking guilty as hell searching every room making sure he didn't have some hoe hiding up in here.

"Tracey, what ya crazy ass doing?" He asked, but I ignored him until I confirmed nobody was in his house.

"Angelo what's going on with us." I finally asked only for his crazy ass to cock his gun back. My eyes widen as I looked at him not in fear, but in shock that he had the audacity to play with me like this.

"You the one moving funny Tracey who the fuck was that texting you, and who the hell you go out to dinner with."

"First of all...'"" Was all I could get out before he cut me off.

"Dead the smart shit that you about say. You already knew what type time I was on when we made this official."

"I went out to eat with Riley she has a new number because Sebastian literally kicked her out of the car ass naked. Than on top of that, he's taking away her business and shit just because she doesn't want to return home. But since you think I'm being foul why the fuck did the bitch Naomi feel the need to wait until I go to the bathroom to speak with you. Then you had that hoe hugging all up on you. I should have cut you and her!"

Hell yeah, I lied nobody had time to deal with the psychotic thoughts going through this fool head. Yes I did flip that shit right on him. That was the main reason why I was piss the day after we ate brunch. I saw the whole situation with him and that girl.

"Are you still fucking her?"

"No… That shit was nothing she just came over to make sure I was good because she knew what that day was." He answered like it justified this hoe hugging on him.

"Angelo don't play with me."

"Babe I ain't never been one to lie." He said putting his gun down on the end table before pulling me closer to him.

"So can we move on from this bullshit I hate the space we are in."

Angelo started intensely in my eyes causing me to feel quite uncomfortable. It seemed like he was trying to read me to see if I was lying. I knew he peeped game and how I flipped everything on him, but it is what it is. We both did some foul shit and Angelo may have never lied to, but this muthafucka knew how to withhold the truth.

"Babe…" I moaned as I put my hand in his boxers.

"Tracey if I find out you lying I'm going to fuck you up." He groaned.

"I'm not." Bending down pulling his boxer along with me; coming face to face with his dick I took him in my mouth. Tonight, was the night we were making up for lost time.

"Hello," I answered my phone grouchily. Last night me and Angelo was having the best make up sex of our lives.

"Hey, baby girl." The voice came through the phone causing me to wake all the way up in the bed.

"Daddy?" I knew my ears were deceiving me. Throughout the past couple months, me and my mother had gotten back on good terms and was rebuilding our relationship. But my father never reach out to me, and when I asked to speak to him, he would always decline.

"Yeah, sweetie did I catch you at a bad time?"

"No! Dad wassup." I asked nervously. Praying that everything was okay with my mother.

"I calling you to see how you were doing," My dad asked and I smiled a mile wide.

"I'm good daddy thanks for asking. Daddy, I'm so sorry."

"I know, and I want to apologize for you too. I was still punishing you when you already were punished by losing five years of your life. I was hurt by your actions because I already knew how this was going to turn out to you. But I realize your just like me, and you will have to live and learn."

"And I have learned. I will never put another man's life before mine. I'm sorry that me going to jail didn't just affect our home life but your work life too." My mother already told me he was passed up on a job because of me.

"That's in the past. I'm on my way to work now. I just wanted to call and ask you out to lunch this Friday." My father asked shocking me, but I was beyond ecstatic.

"Sure daddy I would love that!"

"Great I call you later." He said before hanging up. My morning couldn't get any better.

"Who the hell got you smiling so hard," Angelo asked bringing me breakfast in bed.

"Besides last night and you making me my favorite food this morning. My father called me."

"Word? What he say." Angelo asked as I took the tray of food from him.

"He apologized and invited me to lunch on Friday," I replied

222

before digging into my eggs, bacon, grits, and waffles.

"Where you going?" I asked seeing him get dressed.

"I have some moves to make." He said. I knew he was talking about his business. But his phone kept going off. It was even going off last night, but I was too busy enjoying the feeling he was giving my body to care.

Don't go looking for trouble or asking questions you truly don't want to know the answer too.? I silently thought coaching myself not to bring it to his attention.

"Oh okay. Let me hop in the shower I have to meet with my parole officer today." I said finishing the rest of my breakfast.

"Alright." He said kissing me on the lips.

After walking Angelo to his door, I quickly got in the shower and dressed to head to my parole meeting. I already knew this was going to be quick Officer Tate usually just drug tested me and I be on about my day. Walking inside the parole office downtown. I quietly waited my turn to see Officer Tate.

"Tracey." My name was finally called.

"Hey, girl you know the drill. Just take this test, and I'll have you out of here in no time." Officer Tate said handing me the cup. We walked to the bathroom, and she stood by the door while I went to the bathroom. Coming out of the bathroom she told me to go back into her office while she tested my pee.

"Okay, you passed. Now, Tracey, I have something I have to speak with you about. Things are about to change around here starting after this meeting I will no longer be your parole officer."

"Why." I asked a little upset. Officer Tate was cool people we had our own relationship, and I knew she wasn't about to bull-shit me and drawl like most parole officers. I really didn't feel like starting this process over with a new person.

"Well, I received a better job opportunity in Maryland. So, this is my last week here. However, the Officer that will be taking on your case is good and a dear friend to me." She said and the door open. I swear God had to be playing a fucking joke on me.

"Tracey this is Officer Naomi Sanchez." Officer Tate introduced us.

"Hello, Tracey, nice to meet you," She smirked sneakily, and she held out her hand for me to shake which I hesitantly shook.

"Officer Sanchez... Tracey here will not be a problem. She's the best parolee I had. You can look over her file and see she upstanding and truly working hard to change her life around. I truly admire this lady here." Officer Tate sang my praises, and if I wasn't mistaking, I saw Naomi slightly roll her eyes.

"That's great to hear. The last thing I want is for issues to arise and we have to send you back to jail." Officer Sanchez stated snidely causing Officer Tate too look at her sideways.

"There will never be an issue. I have a great support system. My cousin and man always keep me on the straight and narrow." I winked.

"Are we done here?"

"Yes, Tracey it was nice meeting you, and I wish nothing but success in the future." Officer Tate said giving me a handshake. I genuinely smiled and wished her the same while Naomi hating ass stared a hole through me.

"Tracey I will be in contact with you. I move a little different than Officer Tate. I just want this transition to be as easily as possible.

"Okay" I agreed, before walking out of the officer. I hope Angelo's pass doesn't fuck up my future.

Chapter 28

Desi

"Mommy!" Marcell yelled my name as soon as he saw me walk through my mother's front door. There was no greater joy in the world than spending time with my son. Every day I wake up with regret that I didn't get my act together sooner. My mother Theresa has done a great job raising my son. I could never tell her how much I appreciate her stepping up. Also, allowing me the opportunity to come back in his and her life.

"Hey Mar Mar, you ready to go with mommy!" I said picking him up and spinning him around. Looking into his chocolate face, it was a damn shame he looks just like the man who didn't want him." Hey, momma thanks for letting me take him for the weekend."

"No problem. I'm just happy you're growing up and trying to handle your responsibility." She said nodding her head in Marcell's direction.

When I first started coming around my mom would shut the door in my face. She was dead set on not letting me run in and out of Marcell's life. I completely understood why too; I was a horrible mother. When I got pregnant, I saw me and Mason living and caring for Marcell. But all Mason did was make me abandon him. I did so many foul and grimy things to get Mason back I wasn't gonna to lose him. Looking back, I realize how stupid and selfish I've been. I should have known Mason didn't love me when he had me risking everything making drops and picking up drugs for him. He would have never asked Tracey to do that shit.

That's why when she offered to make the drop that night I convinced him to allow her. All this time I thought Tracey was my problem. Even while this girl was in jail, I hated her because he would always compare me to her or find away to bring her up in a conversation. Do I regret setting Tracey up?. Yea it was fucked up, and I know karma was going to come and bite me in the ass.

"Where's Peanut?" Marcell asked excited to see him. These past couple days Peanut has been nothing short of extraordinary. I hated the fact that I kept playing him to the side for Mason. I always had deep feelings for Peanut, and I'm happy that I acted on them. I know when I first approached Peanut it was on some scheming shit. But seeing him really take a chance on me despite how his cousins feel made me want to stop all of the bullshit; main reason why I been ignoring Mason.

Its no secret in the streets that Angelo caught up with Mason and cut his hand off. When Mason called me from the hospital to let me know what happended. I decided to keep my distance. Mason was going to get me killed one day, and I had a son to live for. Being back in Marcell's life and being Peanut's main girl I did a whole 360. I got me a job at PECO the electric company in the call center making an honest living.

"He's home making us dinner." I smiled. Not only did Peanut love me, but he treated Marcell like he was his son. That's more than I can say for Mason's dumb ass.

"I always liked that boy. He's the one you should have married. Not Mason." My mother let me know. She never shied away from telling me how she really felt about Mason.

"Lesson learned I'm thinking about going to the lawyer and filing for a divorce. I'm really trying hard to change my life around. I want to be a mother to my son. I should have never put you in the position to raise my child. Even though I want to put all of the blame on Mason, I can't. I made the choice to put him before my child. I made the choice to bring Marcell in this world knowing

Mason never wanted kids."

"Having kids don't keep a man. You was trying to compete with a woman who was just as dumb as you over that boy. But I see the growth in you, and I'm not going to throw ya past in your face. I have no problem with you taking your place in Marcell's life. I just want to make sure you are genuine, and this is not a phase. Once I feel like you are one hundred percent ready to take him on full time I will gladly sign my rights over to you. Like you said I should have never been put in the position to raise my grandson in the first place. But I be damned if I let you keep him and you revert back to ya old ways."

Just hearing my mom say she would sign her rights over to me was like music to my ears. I knew I messed up in the past, so I had to play by her rules. But I'm ready for my son to live with me. I'm ready to be a mother.

"I understand mom."

"Mommy you ready to go," Marcell asked impatiently.

"Yeah."

We said our goodbyes to my mother and continued on our way. Before heading straight home, we stopped at the Red Box to rent a couple of movies for the night. This is the first weekend my mom allowed Marcell to stay the night and I was hoping that this could be our regular routine. I've been kind of paranoid lately; I know Mason had something up his sleeve. I basically abandon my mission and been ignoring all of his calls and texts. I wish my greed never brought me to this point. I actually liked working a nine-five. Peanut been so supportive of me and my change that he actually started to let his guard down and telling me things like the codes to the safe in his house. Even though I never took anything I know he had well over one hundred thousand dollars in there.

Peanut was still closed mouth on his business dealings with his cousins. I think that's because he don't fully trust me and his cousin Aquil is crazy as fuck. Aquil is one of the main reasons why

I don't want to set Peanut up. That nigga has a reputation around Philly, and it's not a nice one. He's known to fuck up anything and anyone in his path if they do him or his brother dirty. Peanut already told me to keep my distance when he's around because he thinks my eyes are shifty and if I look at him wrong he's liable to shoot me. See that nigga crazy for real for real.

Walking up to the door of the house I could hear Meek Mills Champions blasting through the surround sound he had set up in the living room. Peanut was always blasting music, so this was nothing new. Pulling out my keys to unlock the door I realized it was already cracked open.

"Baby you left the door unlocked and cracked open," I shouted. Peanut hated when I did that shit, so I found it odd that he would do that himself. I moved further into the house I told Marcell to put in clothes in his bedroom. I followed the smell of the food; he was cooking my favorite steak, mash potatoes, asparagus, and shrimp.

"Peanut...."

"I see you forgot your purpose here." Mason's voice caused me to halt all movement. The sight in front of me brought tears to my eyes. Mason and some other nigga was holding Peanut at gunpoint. Not only were they holding him a gunpoint it looked like they beat him up in the process. I knew all types of emotions and thoughts had been running through Peanut's mind. I hated the truth was about to come out.

"Mason, what are you doing here?" I asked the dumbest question.

"I came here to finish the fucking job you started. You fucked around and fell for the mark." He barked. I knew he was pissed. I don't know if he was upset because I abandoned the job or the fact he could tell me, and Peanut loved one another. I looked at Peanut, and he let out a groan.

"Peanut..." I wanted to explain everything. What Mason was

saying wasn't a lie, but I had a change of heart in this situation.

"Oh, nigga as many jobs as we've pulled off you actually didn't see this as a setup." Mason laughed in Peanut's face making shit worse. Yes, this started out as Peanut being a mark. But things change when I found out that he was still sniffing around Tracey. Yeah, I knew all about their little dinner date, and I wasn't even mad. Here I was once again putting my life on the line for us to survive and he's still chasing after this girl. So, I decided to dead the whole set up thing plus being with Peanut was changing me to a better person.

"Peanut I know you didn't think she really loved you." Peanut just turn his head causing Mason and this unknown man to enjoy his pain.

"Desi get the money, so we can be out," Mason demanded looking at me daring me to disobey.

"Mason just leave," I begged.

"Bitch do what I said before I shoot this muthafucka. What you thought this was? Your dumb ass thought I wouldn't figure out y'all was fucking behind my back."

"You told me to do that." I was now confused. He was the one telling me to do everything in my power to get Peanut off guard. Before this set up he had me selling my body.

"Naw I'm talking about before all of this. This nigga was my best friend. Y'all foul as shit. Now get the money." He said letting off a shot in Peanut's right knee causing him scream out in pain as blood sprayed everywhere.

I rushed into his basement and went directly to the safe. I knew there was no coming back after this Peanut will forever hate me. All my concern was getting me and Marcell out of this safe. Grabbing the duffle bag which was heavy. Opening it up it had to be at least fifty different types of guns inside. I started grabbing all of the money in the safe and throwing it inside the duffle bag. Once the safe was empty,I zipped of the bag and started to drag it up the steps.

POW!

"Oh my God!" I screamed trying to run up the steps. I prayed ason didn't kill Peanut and Marcell was still upstairs.

"What fuck did you just do!" I heard the panic in Mason's voice causing me to move faster not really wanting to face the reality on what was on the other side of the door.

"I didn't know somebody else was in the house. It was an accident. Fuck lets get out of here."

"Nigga you shot my fucking son!" Mason barked I bust through the door and found Marcell laying on the kitchen floor with a bullet in the middle of his head.

"Noooooo!" I dropped the duffle bag and ran to my son. Lifting his lifeless body into my arms, I let out a gut-wrenching scream.

POW!

The gun when off again I prayed I was the attended target. How could I live with Marcell dead; I truly let him down. The other man's body dropped.

"Let's go!" Mason barked picking up the heavy duffle bag and pulling me up. Looking at Peanut I cried even harder my son's death was on my hands and Peanut didn't look like he would be surviving much longer either.

"Why would you do this?"

"Baby I'm sorry I didn't know you had Marcell here," Mason said like that made a difference.

"We have to go. We're about to have bounty out on us."

Knowing he was right. If Peanut cousins didn't come looking for us, I know my mother would send the police when Marcell didn't return. Getting myself together we left the house as quickly as possible. The neighbors were already peaking out of their windows being nosey.

"This can't be my life," I muttered as reality hit we're about to be on the run for the rest of our lives.

Chapter 29

Naomi

"**N**aomi, I care for you. But I love Tracey. Always have and always will. Maybe if I never met her, I could give us a try. But with her in my life that will never happen." Angelo said drunk as hell sitting on my bed

Angelo's words kept running through my mind. His drunk confession had me hating Tracey even more. The whole night he came over drunk all he talked about was Tracey and how this unknown number was texting her number. I thought he would be drunk enough to lose all self-control and sleep with me. I was damn near throwing myself on him, and he never took the bait. Even when he had proof that Tracey was being sneaky and foul, he was still faithful. I never seen myself being crazy over a man, but I truly feel as though Angelo was my soul mate. I tried moving on with Elijah. However, I can't get my mind off Angelo to enjoy him. At the end of the day its not fair to Elijah if I string him along when I know he will never have my heart.

"Are you ready?" Jacobson asked excitedly.

Parole Officer Jacobson was fresh out of college landing a job as parole officer. Today he was my partner for the day as we made an unexpected house visits. We had to do this at least once a month to make sure the parolees were living right and wasn't around drugs, guns, or anything that will lead them back to jail. Tracey was our last visit, and I hated that I had to see this girl's face. I would have never expected that she was on parole, it shocked me but knowing I had her future in my hands made me fill empowered.

"Yeah, this the last one of the day. So, let's make it quick." I said as we left the Applebee's.

My blood boiled as I pulled up in the neighborhood Tracey lived in. These houses were magnificent. Her house was better than mine, and all I knew was Angelo was the one who set her up like this. Why couldn't he love me the way he loved her.

"Are you okay?" Jacobson asked looking at me strangely. I was heated; I didn't even realize he could hear me mumbling things about Tracey and Angelo.

Standing in front of her door was an older gentleman. If he didn't look so much like her, I would have snapped a picture of him and sent it to Angelo. For some reason, he now believes that he was overreacting the night he was drunk. I think he just doesn't want to know the truth. Pulling out my phone I tried to call Angelo, but the message on the phone notified me that this was no longer a working number. How could he change his number once again? Now I have no way of getting in contact with him. I rather a piece of him than nothing at all.

"Daddy!" Tracey came to her door and gave her father a hug.

"Hey, baby girl are you ready for our date." He said. Tracey looked like a little girl on Christmas day in the man's presence.

"Ummm hmmm." I made my presence known as we walked up to her house.

"Hello, Tracey we're here for our monthly visit and inspection," I said.

"Oh, I was on my way out. Daddy this my parole officer." She said letting me know.

"Oh, okay let them do what they came here for, and we can be on our way." He said like they had a choice I was coming up in here regardless of their little plans.

Tracey let us in and my body filled green with envy stepping into her house. It was absolutely gorgeous. On one of the walls in the living room was a blown-up picture of her and Angelo they looked to be teenagers. I would say it was cute if it didn't bring me so much pain.

"Are you going to search the house or look at my pictures. We kind of have reservations." Tracey snapped. I guess I was staring too hard at Angelo.

"Jacobson I will take upstairs and you take downstairs," I ignored Tracey and started to do my job.

"Got you."

I searched every room in this house, and everything was perfect she didn't have any drugs laying around in visible sight nor any firearms. I kind of expected it because her parole officer before me spoke so highly of her. She basically told me I wouldn't have a problem with Tracey. But she was wrong. The man that I love loves Tracey and in my eyes, that was a huge problem. Going against every moral I had in my body I dug inside of my purse and grabbed two Kilos of coke and placed them on the shelf of her walk-in closet in her bedroom. I had to get her out of Angelo's life one way or another. I knew this was a risk. In the end, Angelo probably still wouldn't want anything to do with me. But it was a risk I was willing to take. Either way, Tracey will be out of his life rather he's with me or not.

"What are you doing?" Jacobson's voice boomed scaring me half to death that I knocked one of the kilos of coke on the ground. By the look on his face, I knew he saw what I had just done.

"Tracey!" I ignored him and yelled her name. Tracey and her father both walked into the bedroom.

"Is this little inspection done?"

"Yes, and your being arrested. I found two kilos of coke on your closet shelf." I said in a matter of fact tone with a smirk. That I'm sure, she wanted to smack off.

"What! There were no drug in my house before you walked ya high yellow hating ass up in here. You're trying to set me up!" Tracey snapped trying to charge at me but was stopped by her father.

"Tracey let them arrest you. I will meet you at the precinct." Her father said with a look of disappointment cascading over his face.

"Daddy no this is all about Angelo. She's made that he doesn't want her anymore." Tracey's eyes began to water, and I enjoyed every moment of watching this bitch break.

"Jacobson please do the honors of arresting this girl." I hissed, and Jacobson looked at me with confliction in his heart.

He was a good kid and was good at his job. Now I was about to make him arrest this innocent woman behind my own happiness. At the end of the day, it's always been an unspoken word that your partner will never snitch on you. If they do none of our other co-workers will ever trust them. Making working as a Parole officer hell. Especially, when doing home visits. There are times we may have to use our firearms. There's nothing worse than going into a situation that can turn deadly and know nobody will have your back.

"Tracey Harris, You have the right to remain silent. Anything you say can and will be used against you in a court of law. You have the right to an attorney. If you cannot afford an attorney, one will be provided for you." Jacobson read her, her right before placing his silver handcuffs on her.

"You know Angelo's going to fuck you up." She muttered as I was walking by her.

"Is that a threat," I asked trying to pump fake like the words she just spoke didn't send a chill down my spine.

"Naw, you already know it's a promise." She chuckled as Jacobson escorted her out of her house.

"Where are y'all taking her." Her father asked, and Jacobson rambled off the precinct location that we were taking her too to get booked.

Getting inside of the car I looking through the rear-view mirror and saw the tears running down Tracey's face. But the look in her eyes had me lost for words. I knew I would regret this move in the future.

Chapter 30

Cream

Things had been hectic lately. Brooklyn basically done moved into my condo since she went home and found her house ransacked. She didn't know who was coming for her and that was pissing me off the most. I hated that she had to look over her shoulder. She will never be comfortable until we find this person. I honestly think it could be one of her admirers at the club. Lately, I've been wanting to have a talk with her about stripping. I wanted her to stop period. I know we haven't made anything official, but everybody around that knows me knows she's my girl and not to fuck with her.

The last time I picked her up from KING's all of my lil homies was in there partying. As much as I tried to not make her career a big deal, it's truly bothering me. I don't want other men to see what's mine. Especially, not the niggas that work for me. I know this conversation would probably be the end of us because Brooklyn was all about the paper and getting her to stop stripping was something that she wasn't going to do easily. I must have spoken her up because she was calling my phone.

"Wassup ma," I answered.

"What you want for dinner tonight?"

"Whatever you make is good with me." I couldn't stop the smile creeping on my face if I wanted to. When I offered her to stay with me, it was for her safety.. In the beginning, I let her stay in the condo by herself, and I stayed at my house. I'm a person who always wanted their own space. But I always seemed to find my way over to the condo. Plus, Brooklyn hated when I never came home to her. Every night there was a home cooked meal awaiting me, along with her ready to bust it open without hesitation.

"Alright, I'm feeling like surf and turf tonight. I'll stop by the market and pick up crabs, shrimp, salmon, steak, potatoes, and broccoli."

"Sounds good."

"Did your Aunt hear from your cousin yet?"

"I don't know." I let out a sigh. This wasn't like Blue not to reach out to us.

"I know my mom and her went down there today to see what was going. Now I'm on my way to mom dukes house that's where everybody at."

"So is he okay. Do you want me to meet you there?"

"They won't tell me anything over the phone. All my mom said was get to get there ASAP. But naw do what you was going to do; after I leave her house, I'm coming straight to you."

"Okay, I'll see you later," Brooklyn said before she hung up. The urgency in my mom's voice had me on pins and needles. I'm not even trying to put out any negatives thoughts or energy. But all I know is if something happened to Blue all hell is breaking loose.

"Yo Lo," I answered my phone.

"You already at my mom's house?"

"Naw some fuck shit just happened with Tracey she locked up. Her mom called me crying saying they found drugs in her house when the parole officer came to do a visit."

"Nigga I know you ain't do no rookie shit and leave drug in sis house." I had to ask. I know for a fact Tracey would never do anything that would put her in a predicament to land herself back in jail.

"Hell naw. You know better than to ask me some fuck shit like that. Plus with Naomi being her parole officer I wouldn't do anything that would give Naomi a chance to get her out of my life." He said then the line went silent. I know he didn't just say his old jump off was Tracey's parole officer.

"I'm going to kill that bitch!" He hung up probably on the search for Naomi's hoe ass now. I don't even think she knew what she just done.

Pulling up to my mom's house I could see all of our family cars parked on the blocked. I decided to smoke a blunt before I walked my black ass up in there ready to hear what the hell was going on with Blue. As I smoked I noticed Chantel making her way up to my mother house. Now I knew some fuck shit happened knowing that they called Chantel down here. Chantel was my big sister. Blue loved that girl, and they shared a daughter together.

Let me get out of this car.

Walking up to my mom's house a feeling of sadness came over me. This feel only magnified when I walked inside and saw the look on everybody's face.

"Sawyer..." My mom called me by my name.

"Have a seat."

"What's going on," Chantel asked I could tell she was nervous to hear the news. My Aunt Alberta looked to be in a daze. Like she was on another planet.

"Blue was murdered." My mom could barely get it out before she broke down in my arms.

"They done killed my baby!" My Aunt Berta screamed falling out the chair and onto the floor. This news fucked up my head up. Blue my was more than my cousin he was my brother. The only nigga who was there to teach how to be a man.

"What did they say happen!" I barked. I was pissed why wasn't our family notified.

"They said he was stabbed in the library. Him and another inmate was stab, but the other inmate is still alive. The prison already buried him in the cemetery." My mom muttered.

"I couldn't even say bye to my baby. How could they bury him without even letting me know he died?"

My heart went out to my Aunt; that was some fucked up shit that the prison pulled. But what I wanted to know was why the fuck Mike's bitch ass didn't reach out to me or Angelo to let us know what the fuck happened. He ain't have no problem reaching out to Lo when he spared Mason's life. Walking up to my aunt I kissed her on the forehead and told my mom I would be back.

"Cream what am I going to tell Blu," Chantel sobbed.

"Tell her her daddy loved her." I pulled Chantel into a hug. I couldn't even hold my tears back. Blue was really gone. My fucking OG! He didn't deserve this shit.

"I have to go." Getting in my car. All I did was drive around Philly and smoked another blunt.

Brooklyn: *Baby dinner ready. I'm about to a nap before you come home.*

Pulling up to Kerm's the local bar that we always use to go to and chill. I decided to have a couple drinks for the falling homies. I don't even think I could get over this death. This was a hurt piece. Blue ain't have to worry about Chantel and Blue because I will always hold them down

"Yo Cream, Kerm told me to cut you off. Do you need me call you a ride." Mika, the bartender, asked me. Looking down at my watch I couldn't believe I was sitting her for three hours straight throwing shots of Henny back.

"Naw I'm good shorty," I said standing up and stumbled a little.

"Youngblood where ya car keys you already know I'm not letting you drive like this," Kerm said walking towards me. He was the old head in the neighborhood that we all looked up too. My mom even dated him back in the day.

"How's ya mom? Everybody cool why you in here drinking like a fish?"

"She cool you should hit her up. Blue was murdered while in jail." I said, and he motioned for Mika to pour me another shout.

"Damn." I tossed that shot back and placed the glass back on bar.

"Yo can you drive me home," I asked.

"Yeah, Mika hold things down. I'll be back to lock up."

Getting in the car I gave him my address. He drove in silence as every thought ran through my head. As of now, all I wanted to do is get revenge on whoever took my cousin away from our family. I didn't even tell Angelo about his death. That nigga is going to want to break in the jail just to kill whoever did this to Blue.

"Damn, it look like some shit popping off," Kerm said bringing me out of my thoughts. Looking around there were fire trucks and police cars blocking off the block where my condo was. Getting out the car I could see huge black clouds of smoke.

"Yo, what hell is going on down there?" I asked some young jawns that was walking towards me.

"That condo down the street caught on fire, and some people are trapped inside." She said before walking away.

"Fuck Brooklyn!" I hauled ass down the street with people trying to pull me back. The last thing I knew was Brooklyn texted me she was taking a nap.

God, please tell me she got out safe I can't take another loss today

To be Continued...

CPSIA information can be obtained
at www.ICGtesting.com
Printed in the USA
LVHW080610300120
645191LV00007BA/242